A CANDLELIGHT ECSTASY ROMANCE

"It can all end right now, if that's what you want."

"That's not what I want."

He gave her his open mouth, and her freed hands flew to catch his bare shoulders and back. With a deliberation that was maddening, he wound the futile little strings around his fingers until they snapped, and the thin cloth that separated her flesh from his dropped away. As he explored and memorized every turn, curve, and dip of her body, her need became an ache that burned both of them. She arched herself upward, moaning under the pressure of his hunger.

Then, vaguely, she sensed that they were not alone.
. . .

1　THE TAWNY GOLD MAN, Amii Lorin
2　GENTLE PIRATE, Jayne Castle
3　THE PASSIONATE TOUCH, Bonnie Drake
4　THE SHADOWED REUNION, Lillian Cheatham
5　ONLY THE PRESENT, Noelle Berry McCue
6　LEAVES OF FIRE, FLAME OF LOVE, Susan Chatfield
7　THE GAME IS PLAYED, Amii Lorin
8　OCEAN OF REGRETS, Noelle Berry McCue
9　SURRENDER BY MOONLIGHT, Bonnie Drake
10　GENTLEMAN IN PARADISE, Harper McBride
11　MORGAN WADE'S WOMAN, Amii Lorin
12　THE TEMPESTUOUS LOVERS, Suzanne Simmons

Dear Reader:

In response to your enthusiasm for Candlelight Ecstasy Romances, we are now increasing the number of titles per month from two to three.

We are pleased to offer you sensuous novels set in America depicting modern American women and men as they confront the provocative problems of a modern relationship.

Throughout the history of the Candlelight line, Dell has tried to maintain a high standard of excellence, to give you the finest in reading pleasure. It is now and will remain our most ardent ambition.

Vivian Stephens
Editor
Candlelight Romances

DESPERATE LONGINGS

Frances Flores

A CANDLELIGHT ECSTASY ROMANCE

Published by
Dell Publishing Co., Inc.
1 Dag Hammarskjold Plaza
New York, New York 10017

Dell ® TM 681510, Dell Publishing Co., Inc.

ISBN: 0-440-12831-5

Printed in the United States of America
First printing—June 1981

CHAPTER ONE

Perched on the side of the mountain on their thin, exposed foundations, the houses above seemed doomed to slip crazily down to the bottom of Coldwater Canyon.

Luz Rivas captured the long strands of her dark hair with a graceful tug and leaned to gaze up out of the car window again. "I couldn't live in one of those houses. They don't look safe to me. Besides," she said with absolute conviction, "I think they're ugly!"

Her companion at the wheel frowned. "Don't be stupid! The view of Los Angeles from the top of that hill is fantastic." The frown deepened, and Rita Campos took her eyes off the winding road just long enough to give her friend an anxious, critical glance. "Those houses cost a fortune, and some very successful people in the film industry live up there, you know!"

"I know," Luz replied, barely keeping the exasperation out of her voice. "You're suddenly impressed by expensive homes and 'very successful people,' aren't you, Rita?"

"Yes, I am!" the girl snapped. "Aren't you?"

"No. I work at the studio every day with 'very successful people' and I find most of them to be terribly self-centered and sometimes even boring."

Rita kept her eyes glued on the narrow road curving and twisting through the wooded base of the canyon, but her hands began to shake in spite of the fact that they were tightly wrapped around the rim of the wheel. "Why do you always say such outrageous things?"

"You've got it all wrong," Luz protested. "I'm simply being honest."

"Honest?" Rita asked explosively. "I suppose the next thing you're going to tell me is that you actually prefer living in our old overcrowded neighborhood in East Los Angeles, right?"

"You know I love it."

That remark brought forth a loud, sarcastic laugh of disbelief from Rita. "You've got to be kidding me! How can you enjoy living squeezed in among those dreary, tacky, little stucco houses all filled with gossipy, nosy neighbors yakking away in Spanish?"

Luz shook her head thoughtfully. Why was it that lately every word, every conversation between them always seemed to lead directly into an argument? This particular subject was cropping up with an infuriating regularity. "I loved the *barrio* when I first saw it as a frightened, lonely ten-year-old arriving from Mexico"—Luz's bewitching brown eyes grew soft remembering—"and I guess I'm still unsophisticated enough to feel comfortable living in my sister's tiny house, yakking away with the *friendly* neighbors in Spanish." She couldn't help adding pointedly, "The old gossips only get vicious when somebody gives them something juicy they can really dig their teeth into."

"Oh, so now you're going to preach to me! I hate it when you're in one of your self-righteous goody-goody-girl moods, Luz." Rita's eyes, as dusky and dazzling as Luz's, sparked with anger. Her harsh expression emphasized the marked differences between the two girls, too. Although both had the beautiful coloring of their *mestizo* Mexican-Spanish heritage, Luz unconsciously had allowed her loveliness to remain unspoiled while Rita had recently resorted to dying the tips of her sheared hair a chic silver that looked as unnatural as the exaggerated, dramatic makeup she insisted on wearing. Now the harshness crept into her voice as well as her features. "And I hate the *barrio,* too. You may stay and rot in it—but I can't wait to get out of it!"

"Why?" Luz asked, truly concerned. "You were born in East L.A. and you grew up there just as I have. Why do you suddenly hate it so much?"

"I've gotten the chance to see how the better half of the world lives . . ."

"You mean you've seen how *this* half of the world lives," Luz suggested, tilting her head up toward the soaring glass palaces on the hill, "so now you're itching to be a part of the so-called smart studio set, right?"

"That's right," Rita answered defensively, "and what's so wrong about wanting to get out of the *barrio?*"

"Nothing—unless you let yourself become just another tragic statistic in this trendy part of town."

"Oh, sure, that's easy for you to say because you're the brainy type and you've gotten all the breaks," Rita hissed, venting a secret resentment she had probably carried around for a long time. "*You* had the chance to go to college, and *you* graduated with honors, so *you* were sitting pretty when that fancy job at Mercury Studios opened up." She kept her eyes pinned to the road, concentrating fiercely. "I barely made it through secretarial school, but I'm smart enough to know I have to make my own breaks —and grab all the happiness I can while I'm still young."

"But that doesn't mean you have to turn completely away from your background and traditions . . ."

"Traditions!" scoffed Rita, making the word sound dirty somehow. "That's what you may call all those stupid outdated customs, but I call them chains and shackles. I'm sick and tired of the whole scene!" Her eyes surprisingly filled with tears.

Enough, Luz thought. In another moment Rita would be crying and the ghastly scene that had occurred earlier

9

this evening would start all over again. *Quick, change the subject,* she told herself. "I have to admit the area around here is very beautiful. It's hard to believe we're right in the middle of a city of millions of people, isn't it?" She peeked over at Rita and continued to talk fast, keeping her voice light and airy. "This canyon looks like a forest out in the middle of nowhere."

"We're not out in the middle of nowhere," Rita replied impatiently. "In fact, we're right in the middle of Hollywood, and we're on our way to Chuck Harrison's house to have a great time, aren't we?" She guided the car expertly around a wicked curve. "Well, aren't we?"

"Yes, Rita, I know. I promised I would try to have a great time tonight and I meant it."

Luz had lied out of sheer desperation; she dreaded the hours ahead. Despite her workaday experience in the movie industry she still felt uncomfortable socializing with certain types of studio people. She simply did not fit in with Rita's new friends and their casual afterwork Hollywood scene, and she was miserable whenever she tried to fake having a "great time." Some part of her early convent breeding still stuck to her spirit, and it wouldn't allow her to give in to the wild nightlife or the brittle glitter that so often caused bitter disappointment and pain. In an industry where casting couches, bitchery, and body-trading could make some careers possible, Luz's native sense of honesty, more than false modesty or actual prudery, prevented these methods from ever crossing her mind.

The soft Southern California night wove its magic into the air but did nothing to brush away Luz's apprehension about tonight. God! Why hadn't she resisted when Rita had dragged her off to what would probably turn out to be one of those usually predictably loathsome studio parties with "very successful people"!

Rita's tears had miraculously disappeared. She flashed a tight, artificial smile. *"¡Que bueno, chica!* I'm glad you've decided to act human like everybody else, because I don't want to spend the evening worrying about you. I just want to relax and have a fantastic time."

Luz didn't bother to answer. She knew what lay ahead; too much noise, too much drinking, and too many familiar tales of studio intrigues told by the same people. But she knew Rita wouldn't be bored. Rita had been swiftly captivated by the dazzle of this particular Hollywood lifestyle right from the first moment Luz had found her a job at Mercury Studios as a secretary. Unfortunately, Rita had soon become Chuck Harrison's secretary, and there was suddenly something harmful, even sinister happening to her best friend . . . and Luz had a suspicion that the cause of it all was Chuck Harrison.

As if to confirm the suspicion, Rita returned to the only theme that seemed to grip her mind lately. "Chuck throws the wildest, craziest parties in town. He's the most fabulous man I've ever known!"

"Perhaps," Luz murmured cautiously. "I've never actually met him, but . . ."

Rita interrupted quickly. "But—*what?*"

"Nothing, really." To be fair, Luz only knew Chuck Harrison by reputation, but by *all* accounts his was a very foul, tainted reputation. Everybody described him as an offensive, self-indulgent, brutal egomaniac. His sexual exploits were the basis for most of the gossip around the studio where he was the casting director, and his lurid boasts about the many women he bedded filtered down even to Luz's office, which was usually the last department to receive *any* news.

Rita had a good idea of what was twirling around in Luz's mind, so she seized the offensive and attacked quickly. "Do you know what your problem is, Luz? You're a snob. You think no man is good enough for you." She stopped talking just long enough to steer the car sharply off the main road to follow a side street up the face of the

11

mountain. "If you don't stop being so choosy and start having some fun, you're going to be a bitter, frustrated old maid before you're thirty!" She flung Luz a challenging glance. "Admit it—if I hadn't begged you to come with me tonight, you would have spent the whole evening cuddled up with a pile of scripts, reading your eyes out, right?"

Luz nodded, but kept the hurt to herself. *Now* who was guilty of preaching? Her pride saved her for the moment, however, "That's right. I accepted the promotion to senior script analyst knowing I would have to assume an extra work load, so I have no complaints."

"But, it's not *normal* to work *all* the time!"

Luz's control finally snapped. "And I suppose it's *normal* to spend all my time running after muscle-bulging animals like you do, right?"

"That's one hell of a way of putting it, but *yes,* that's what I mean."

"In that case, *no thanks.* I'm not interested." She didn't relish the idea of a series of one-night stands. But perhaps she wasn't being fair to either Rita or Chuck. Deciding to put off condemning the man before she could draw her own conclusions after she met him, some nameless compulsion urged her to turn to her friend, pleading to be heard. "Oh, Rita, can't you tell me what's really bothering you? Can't we still talk about our problems the way we always have?" They had happily shared almost all of their experiences since childhood: school, friendships, secrets, emotions. Until lately . . . until Rita had begun working for Chuck Harrison. "You've been seeing Chuck after work, haven't you, Rita? In fact, you've been dating him a lot, am I right?"

A haunted, wretched look spread across Rita's face, and the tears returned to blur her vision. She impatiently brushed them away with the back of her hand.

"I know you think he's very exciting, and he must live

12

a very glamorous life, but"—Luz blurted out her true feelings before she could stop herself—"before you let yourself become seriously involved with any man . . ."

"How would you know how I feel about Chuck? What do you know about men, or life? *You*—with your scripts, and your books, and your nose always up in the air . . . !"

"Rita, please . . ."

"Shut up, do you hear me! I don't want to talk about it. You wouldn't understand."

"But why not?"

"Because I don't care what he is—I'm in love with him, damn it!"

Luz actually felt sick for a moment. *I don't care what he is,* Rita had cried. So most of the stories were probably true. How could Rita—or any woman with even one ounce of pride—allow herself to fall in love with such an overt, loudmouthed stud?

Rita's tears finally did brim over. "Oh, Luz, please forgive me. I didn't mean to scream at you like that. It's just that I love him so much . . . !"

"Hush, Rita. Please, don't cry," Luz begged, reaching over and hugging her friend. "I understand—I really do." *And I feel very sorry for you,* she almost said. It all added up now: Rita's unusual nervousness; the sudden moods; the waspish, sarcastic answers to even the most simple questions. Chuck Harrison!

"Let's not argue anymore, Luz. Let's talk about this some other time, okay?"

"Of course."

"We're almost at Chuck's house!" The stark yearning in Rita's voice made Luz wince. "Are you really sure this dress looks nice?" the distraught girl asked for the tenth time, restlessly smoothing out the tiny creases that had formed down along her round, shapely legs.

Luz forced herself to smile. "Yes, stop worrying. You

13

look lovely." And hard as nails, too, she might have added. So this was the effect men like Chuck Harrison had on women! Disgusted and sick at heart, Luz finally understood the underlying reason for the horrible, hysterical scene Rita had pulled earlier this evening.

A hasty dinner of various *antojitos* had been served, eaten, and cleared away quickly because Luz's sister, Trina, had been anxious to get to the neighborhood theater where the latest films from Mexico were shown—Trina Rivas's only known vice. Luz had gratefully looked forward to a quiet night alone in the house. She had just scooped up a pile of scripts, preparing to spend the evening working, when the telephone rang. Feeling slightly annoyed at the interruption, she had been astounded to hear Rita's voice on the other end, crying, screaming, and begging Luz to come over to her house *immediately!* It had taken Luz only a second to run down the block to where Rita lived with her widowed mother and a large brood of younger brothers and sisters. Luz politely stopped to greet Mrs. Campos, but Rita's mother, a good woman who was fighting hard to keep her fatherless family together, only shook her head and started to cry. A moment later, Luz had found Rita in her small, cramped bedroom, weeping and frenzied, clothes and shoes thrown around the room, and the expensive dress purchased especially for the party ripped and torn. Sobbing, Rita had resisted all of Luz's frantic efforts to calm her down. *None* of her clothes fit—everything she owned was *ugly,* Rita had screamed. Barely controlling her own frazzled nerves, wondering why Rita was acting like a lunatic, Luz had finally talked her friend into wearing something else. Perhaps the silver harem dress? Yes, Luz had soothed, yes, the silvery material would match the frosting in Rita's hair so well! At long last, Luz had accomplished a miracle, and Rita had put on the tissue-thin dress. Since the anguish and tears had taken up a great deal of time, Rita suddenly realized she was already late for the party—and the tears had begun to flow again. Puzzled, not daring to ask questions and shocked over Rita's bizarre behavior, Luz had foolishly given in to the girl's pleas that she was too upset to go to the party *alone!* Luz *must* be a love and give her moral support—she would fall *apart* if Luz didn't go with her . . . !

Now, Luz carefully studied her companion's flashy but stunning appearance, then peered down at her own simple dark dress. Maybe she should have worn something brighter, something a little less severe? But she hadn't dared to risk another hysterical outburst by taking the time to choose something else, so she had decided to go in her dependable little basic dress. She had hastily brushed out her raven-black hair and now it just fell free around her shoulders, as usual. Why worry how she looked, Luz mused. What difference did it make, anyway!

They reached the crest of the hill and started to approach a long driveway. Rita maneuvered the car through an imposing stone gate and into a narrow private road. The immense, one-story house came into view between towering cypress trees that lined both sides of the drive. Most of the walls of the spectacular building were made of glass and were bare of curtains, with raw steel supporting columns left uncovered. Everything visible had a very high-tech look about it. The rooms hugged the form of the hill like a series of giant building blocks, and its extreme modern shape contrasted with the other canyon houses, mostly built in the "early-nothing" style. Rita braked quickly as the driveway suddenly curved to end in a large courtyard facing the house.

"Good evening, Miss Campos," smiled the virile-looking parking attendant, reaching to open the door of Rita's battered coupe with the same finesse he would have lavished on a Rolls. His red uniform was tight and sexy, leaving very little to the imagination.

"Hi, Davey," Rita smiled familiarly. "How's the party going?"

"Hot, as usual!"

Another equally attractive attendant helped Luz out of the car. Rita greeted him by name, too, then she took Luz's arm and pulled her to the entry doors that reached clear to the top of the roof, flanked by two vertical beams of gleaming stainless steel.

"Still not impressed?" Rita asked sarcastically.

Luz gazed around. The parking attendants had been hired from the most exclusive agency in Beverly Hills, the courtyard was jammed with exotic European cars, larger than life-sized statues of nude gods and goddesses stood bathed in orange lights—all of it spelled MONEY, but little else. She had seen prefab sets at the studio lot that looked less artificial.

Rita mistook her silence for awe. "Just wait until you see the inside of the house. You'll really be speechless!"

I'll bet, thought Luz. The doors were opened almost magically by another attendant in skin-tight red and the deafening assault of blasting disco blotted out any need to respond. She found herself in a foyer melodramatically decorated in tones of gray. The plush carpet beneath her feet felt as luxurious as mink. Every wall was lighted indirectly from the ceiling. The din of the music grew louder and louder as she followed Rita down an iron staircase finally terminating in a room pulsating with human excitement. Obviously, Rita was no stranger either to the staff or to the house. People covered the spaces like brightly painted ants. Some were draped over the uniform pieces of crushed gray velvet furniture, lounging in absolute luxury, while others were propped against the muted walls. Some had arranged themselves in poses along the black Lucite floor. All were in constant motion, talking, laughing, gesturing to one another in spite of the storm of the music.

Luz stopped Rita's swift progress through the press of people with a sharp tug, spinning her friend around. "All right, I give up—what is it?"

Dominating the entire room was a sculpture of hundreds of plumbing pipes, each piece bent and twisted, everything poking out in different directions. It was big, it was vulgar, and it was by far the ugliest piece of junk Luz had ever seen.

"Stop staring like a *ranchera,*" Rita whispered, although the stupefying noise could have drowned out a shout. "It's a very expensive work of art. Chuck had it made in New York by an important SoHo artist." Along with this information came a devastating look of warning. "I think Chuck has the most perfect taste in everything."

"Really?" Luz replied, feeling just annoyed enough by Rita's gushing adulation to react honestly. "Sorry, but I don't think much of his taste in art." She looked carefully around the room at the self-absorbed narcissistic mob of "beautiful people." "I don't think much of his taste in people, either."

But Rita wasn't listening . . . her eyes were searching the room fervently for someone. Suddenly, she found him. Her rapture was like an explosion that shook her whole body.

Chuck Harrison wove his way deliberately, easily, through the crowd, taking his time. He stopped a few tantalizing inches away from Rita. "You took your own damned sweet time getting here, didn't you, baby?"

She shrunk back, stung by his reproach. "I'm sorry. Please don't be angry."

He teased her for another beat or two, then he decided to be forgiving. His brawny arms shot out possessively and then he swung Rita effortlessly off her feet as if she were a doll. It was a showy, calculated maneuver. Everybody around laughed and made the proper, cute remarks. He was the center of attention, and he loved it. Rita shivered,

17

delighted to be so near him. He was wearing a hand-loomed Indian madras shirt provocatively unbuttoned to the waist, and Rita buried her face in the rough abundant hair on his chest like a homing pigeon ecstatically finding its way back to the nest. Luz closed her eyes from the sight.

"How come you're late?" he demanded to know, nibbling away at Rita's earlobe.

"It was all Luz's fault," Rita said, instantly. "She simply couldn't decide what to wear!"

Luz was stunned by this sad, unnecessary lie. She cast her friend a painful glance, but Rita wouldn't meet her eye.

Chuck stopped mouthing Rita's ear long enough to beam a well-practiced grin at Luz. "That was very naughty of you, little girl. I may never forgive you." His tone was bantering, and the full lips curved up in an exaggerated grimace of unbearable frustration.

"I shall probably never forgive myself, either." Even though Rita didn't deserve this kindness, Luz went along with the charade.

Rita finally came out of her daze. "Oh, you two haven't met, have you?"

"Of course, we've met!" Chuck laughed. "You're Luz Rodriguez, right?"

"No. I'm Luz Rivas." Spanish names probably sounded alike to him and "Rodriguez" had been a good guess.

"Oh, yeah, sure, I remember now. You're the head boss in program planning."

"No. I'm senior story analyst in the script department." Why not just admit they had never met before? Luz wondered. Then she realized he was running true to form . . . in this town, everybody always pretended to know everybody else.

His comeback was instant and skillful. "So you're the little genius who's responsible for all those lousy rewrites.

18

I'm playing hell casting my latest film because the roles are different every time I read the script!" What he really meant was: Play the game, honey—don't show me up!

Luz wasn't the least bit intimidated. "Wrong again. I just read them—I don't write them."

It was hard to tell if the smile left his eyes as well as his mouth because of the heavy bronze lenses that stylishly hid the top part of his face. Luz didn't bother to hide the fact that she was openly studying him. She immediately noticed the sharp contrast between the blond gleam of his hair, beard, and mustache, and Rita's dark Hispanic coloring. They made a pretty pair, and she was sure he knew it. Although on the wrong side of forty, she guessed he worked hard to keep his frame in top shape by sweating away hours on racquet and tennis courts, or at an exclusive male fitness center being tortured by weight machines.

Aware he was irritated by Luz's bluntness, Rita tried to smooth over the tension. She pouted, slipped her arms around his waist and took a tiny bite out of his shoulder. The trick certainly worked.

"Hey, somebody get this bright little gal a drink," he bellowed above the rumble, nodding toward Luz, "and keep her amused, because," his voice now dropped theatrically into a sexy growl, "something tells me I'm going to be very busy for the next hour or so . . . !" His lips and hands started to roam all over Rita again.

Watching her friend so eagerly responding to Chuck's expert caresses, Luz suddenly wondered why Rita had asked her to come to this party. Was it because she had a fundamental need to show off in front of Luz, prodded by some perverse female malice? Or had she really desperately needed moral support, frightened and terribly unsure of her hold on Chuck?

Somebody handed Luz a tall chilled glass filled with a frothy orange concoction. She automatically turned and thanked the man. She didn't know him, but he wore the required designer offbeat clothes, and he sported the required deep tan. When his fingers began exploring across her shoulders and down her back, she expected that, too. Noticing how smoothly Chuck was guiding the willing Rita toward what was probably the bedroom, she suddenly felt very weary.

"Thanks for the drink." She shrugged the man's hand off her shoulder, not angrily, just matter-of-factly.

"Oh, come on, darling," the man coaxed, "I can't amuse you if you don't meet me halfway."

"Don't waste your time," she replied, walking away. "I'm not that easily amused." She smiled over her shoulder at him, anyway. "But thanks again for the drink."

His roughish wink implied how easily he could forgive and forget; he was already searching around for a new playmate.

Getting out of that room was not a simple task, but Luz managed somehow. Here and there, as she struggled to cross the room, people recognized her and waved her over. She waved back, smiled pleasantly, and avoided the traps. Air! She had a maddening need for air and silence. The house seemed to be a maze of rooms with wall-to-wall bodies frenetically gyrating to the throb of the music. One room had been specifically set aside as a discothèque. Multicolored lights had been electronically connected to the central stereo and blinding arcs of red, blue, purple, and green responded to the exact beat, casting a weird pattern of colors over the undulating bodies. The whole unreal scene vibrated with sensuality. Many of the men had shed their shirts, revealing compact torsos laced with moisture from the heat of the dancing. The women also appeared to be gripped by the hypnotic invitation of the music. Their beautiful bodies would come into contact with their partners only sporadically, however, every touch singed with undisguised sexuality. Luz actually gasped in disbelief when she saw one of the studio's ordinarily cool, composed receptionists strip down to bikini briefs—and only a gold chain was left to decorate her breasts.

Gathering her wits, Luz finally edged her way beyond the tangle of arms and legs. Directly in front of her loomed a series of sliding glass doors. She pushed against one of them and found herself outside, at last. Gratefully, thirstily, she took a deep breath. The noise from inside the house was only a muted hum now, and there was no one in sight.

She was in a huge garden. The lawn, dotted with exotic plants and flowers that looked ridiculously out of place here in Southern California, where only cacti and succulents grew naturally, looked almost artificial in its perfection. She stepped out on it, half-expecting the grass to be made of plastic turf, but no, it was really natural grass. The garden stretched to the very edge of the hill, then gave way, sloping downward in a sheer drop.

Beneath her gaze, seemingly to infinity, radiated the million flickering lights of Los Angeles. The towers of Century City and the many high-rise buildings along Wilshire's Miracle Mile stood like giant birthday candles amid the miles and miles of illuminated flatland that finally ended at the velvety darkness of the Pacific far, far in the distance. Dominating everything were the lifelines of this incredible sight . . . continuous, never-ending ribbons of luminosity that marked the paths of the famous, or infamous, freeways.

Gone swiftly was the weariness; instead, Luz could feel a rush of the familiar excitement she felt whenever she viewed the endless panorama of this city. By leaning over ever so carefully and using a dash of imagination to spot the different areas, she could trace the important events of her young life. Past the greenery of Griffith Park over to the left were the soft comfortable hills of the *barrios,* still her home, still her security base. To the right, housed in acres and acres of lushness, was the campus of UCLA

21

where she had studied journalism, which she had always loved, and cinema, which finally completely captivated her mind. And almost directly in line, straight ahead, was the glistening superstructure containing the executive offices of Mercury Studios. Rita had been right about one thing, at least. Landing a job with that entertainment empire had been a lucky break. But it hadn't been *all* luck; when the chance had come, she had been prepared. And she had worked very hard to advance to the good position she now held at the studio.

The thought of Rita intruded into her peace like a nagging wound. Luz wondered what to do: should she hang around and wait for Rita, or should she go home, right now? Then she realized she was trapped; they had come to this crazy party in one car!

Luz turned away, her happy mood shattered. A side path beckoned, and she idly followed it until it brought her to the side of a swimming pool the size of a tropical lagoon. Thankfully, there was no crowd cavorting and splashing around; only some plastic pool toys bobbed on the calm surface of the blue-lit water, looking altogether garish and silly. The largest of these artificial sea creatures was a saucy smiling shark. Its very long, very sexy eyelashes caused Luz to grin in spite of her dark mood. The calm, soothing water looked so inviting, and she could have sworn the silly toy shark actually winked an invitation. While debating with herself, she found she was still holding the chilled glass in her hand; she had completely forgotten about it. She set the glass down on the decking and gave in to the childish impulse. Slipping her shoes off quickly, she sat and swung her legs over the side of the pool. Her feet dangled freely in the cool water; it felt delicious. Wiggling her toes back and forth, she watched as the plastic shark came closer and closer. Playfully, her feet and legs sparkling with droplets of spray, she nudged at the creature's wet, soft nose and laughed as it seemed to shyly back away. Repeating this senseless game again and again, she suddenly realized that the spray might drench her dress. Since there was no one around to see, she lifted the hemline and tucked it tightly around her hips. Meanwhile, the toy had been seized by a small current, and it began to drift away toward the far side of the pool as if totally bored by such aimless, human games.

Luz felt the depression she had been attempting to ignore all evening finally taking over. Why on earth was she wasting her time like this? What was she doing here, anyway?

"¿Y tú, niña, qué estas haciendo aquí?"

Luz froze. Was it possible that somebody had been watching her all this time? She glanced around quickly, but she couldn't see anyone else in the garden. Of all the ridiculous situations she had ever encountered, this had to take the prize! Her hands flew to her hips ready to cover her legs, but she stopped, more confused than embarrassed. The resonant male voice had spoken to her in the easy, lilting Spanish of the native Angelino and had exactly repeated her own thoughts: what was she doing here, indeed!

Luz decided definitely not to panic and kept her feet dangling in the water, but her eyes still searched through the darkness. She played for time by taking a sip from the discarded glass at her side. It tasted too sweet, and she hurriedly set the glass down again.

Whoever was sitting out there in the shadows seemed to be waiting for an answer. *"¡No sé!"* she replied honestly, underscoring her own doubts with a shrug, wondering why she felt compelled to carry on this unusual conversation. "What do you think I should do?" she laughed, hoping to bait this stranger out of his lair. "Should I stay, or should I go home?"

He moved then, coming out of the shadows near the edge of the hill, and sat down on the decking quite close to her. Although the obscure light still blurred his features, the reflection from the water showed enough of his face so that she could see it was molded with the fine bones of his Azteca forebears.

"The first thing you should do is to get rid of this," he said with marked disgust, picking up the rejected glass and tossing its contents into a bed of oriental ferns nearby. Then he refilled her glass halfway with wine from his own glass. "I don't think you're old enough to be legally drinking, but let me give you some good advice, anyway. Unless you enjoy waking up in the morning feeling awful, stay away from those sugary mixed drinks and stick to the straight stuff, or wine." He handed over her glass with a mocking glint in his eye.

At least, Luz thought she saw a glitter in his eyes. She wasn't sure because of the thick cast of his dusky, unbelievably long lashes.

"I've been out of college for five years," she informed him, drinking some of the wine, "and I can assure you, everything I do is quite legal."

His smile came slowly, but it was a genuine response. His identity eluded Luz, but recognition wasn't the only reason she quite openly was studying him. He seemed to be easygoing, a quality so often missing in males as stunningly handsome as he certainly was. And confident, too. He *knew* he didn't need tons of gold jewelry and jazzy, punky clothes to set off his extremely masculine Latino appearance.

"But you haven't answered my question, *Luz Rivas* —what the hell are you doing at this kind of bash? And why do you dislike Chuck Harrison so much?"

"Someone should exorcise you!" she gasped, really shaken out of her composure. "How do you know my name?"

"I'd like to impress you and say I possess all kinds of mysterious powers, but"—again that slow, breathtaking smile highlighted his words—"I was there in the room when you and Chuck's latest conquest came in, and I overheard some of the conversation, that's all." This time he laughed in outright admiration. "I have to hand it to you. You really pinned big, bad Chuck's ears back!"

"Chuck's 'latest conquest,' as you call her, is my best friend. The only reason I'm here is because Rita asked me to come." His words had stung, so she had replied with resentment. "I suppose it's because of Rita and the way Chuck— I mean, it's because of Rita that I find myself distinctly disliking Chuck Harrison." Having spoken her mind, she peered up at his face. It was a fascinating face. She was certainly a fool. What if this stranger was a good friend of Chuck's? And who was he, anyway?

"I see." He didn't bother to apologize; the way he spoke the two words, he didn't have to.

"Now may I ask *you* something?"

He merely nodded, but his eyes never seemed to want to leave her face.

"Why were you alone out here in the garden? Don't you like parties?"

"Some parties, yes. And . . . I decided to take a stroll when my date decided to strip off all her clothes," he answered very seriously, but something in his dark eyes sparkled.

Luz remembered the uninhibited receptionist. "Don't you like a woman who strips off all her clothes?"

"You bet I do, but not when she's dancing with another man."

Their combined laughter was quickly muffled by the disturbing arrival of a crowd from inside, shrieking for the stereo to be turned up even louder so that they could dance out by the pool. Swearing softly, he finished his wine, took Luz's glass out of her hand, and deposited both glasses at the base of the ferns. Then he abruptly stood up, pulling her up with him. They were standing only inches apart

25

when a sheet of water came shooting out of the pool as one of the dancers took a belly flop into the water. Luz took the worst of the drenching. She gasped and twisted right into his arms and neither of them moved for a few seconds.

"You'll catch pneumonia unless you dry off," he said rather softly, misunderstanding her slight tremble for a chill as she leaned against him. Or, did he? He spotted a pile of beach towels on a nearby patio table. "Come over here," he said, leading her to a chair and away from the pool, where the rest of the mob had decided to jump in, screaming and splashing. Luz took one of the towels and draped it around her shoulders, drying her damp hair with the ends of the cloth. Her feminine vanity was as limp as her dress. Oh, this was horrible; she must look a mess!

He watched her, guessed her feelings, but managed to remain quite solemn. "Sit down," he ordered. She did, too chagrined to protest. Numb with surprise, she kept very still as he knelt down and began to gently rub her legs with another of the fleecy towels. His head was bent and she could see the tiny drops of water that flocked his dark glossy hair, hair even darker than her own. The same pattern of spray dotted his velvet jacket, covering a body that was slim but as strong as steel. She knew; she had pressed her own body against that strength only a few moments ago. The urge to reach out and flick away the spray while touching his hair, neck, and shoulders was so strong, so insane that she squeezed her hands together tightly, holding them rigid in her lap.

"I think I'll leave the rest to you," he smiled, stopping just at her thighs. He stood up rather quickly, walked over to the pool, and returned with her shoes. They were soaked. "Do you mind walking around barefooted?"

"No, I actually prefer it."

"Good. Let's get out of here."

"Wait!" All of a sudden she remembered Rita—and she felt an immediate pang of remorse. At least Rita had known Chuck for a while before she had given in to his dubious charm. The realization that she herself felt such an acute yearning to waltz off into the night with a man who was a complete stranger actually shocked her more than any dousing of cold water ever could. "I don't even know your name!"

"That's right, you don't. I'm Mario Maldonado."

"The director? But that's impossible . . . !"

"I'm surprised you recognized my name." He examined Luz's face, puzzled by her expression. "What's the matter, are you allergic to film directors?"

"You're so young!"

"In years, maybe, but I've never experienced that luxury. I grew up old."

A strange answer! Luz realized *she* wasn't making much sense, either. "I'm trying to say that I've seen your films many times. They're so beautiful and so sensitive that I just assumed Mario Maldonado was somebody older."

"I haven't made a commercial film yet, so you have to be talking about the documentaries I've been filming for the Chicano Artists' Guild." He looked at Luz rather dubiously. "None of those films have been shown at your friendly commercial movie theater. Where did you see them?"

"I went to a screening of Latino new-wave films at the county Museum of Art last year and that's where I saw one of your documentaries for the first time. I was intrigued, so I went to see another of your films," she admitted without a trace of coyness. "Since then I've caught up with them wherever they're shown—at museums, colleges, or at some of the avant-garde theaters we have around this town. Many people know your work and your name, too. In fact, your films have rather a large cult following."

"So I've heard." He said it without a trace of ego,

obviously perfectly at ease with her honest assessment of his professional talent.

It was inconceivable that he hadn't been contracted to direct a major studio film yet, so Luz asked, "Are you going to continue making only documentaries?"

That marvelous smile returned. "As a matter of fact . . ."

Whatever he was about to say was drowned by an explosion of high screeches and shouts from the almost-nude water nymphs and their hyperactive boyfriends. With a directness that left her little time to protest, he reached out and took her tightly by the hand, then led the way through the labyrinth of the garden. The house was carefully avoided, and soon Luz felt the sponginess of the lawn give way to the pebbles of the driveway. She flinched, not only because of the hurt the stones inflicted on her bare feet, but because she also felt a pinch of conscience about leaving Rita without a word of explanation. Another detail was beginning to gnaw at her, too.

"Sorry," he frowned, "I forgot you weren't wearing shoes. Well, I guess I'll just have to carry you to my car."

His arm had circled her back and he was about to pick her up when Luz stiffened. "Mario, where are we going?"

"Does it matter?"

"Yes." She did not avoid looking directly at him. "For reasons I don't expect you to understand—it matters very much to me."

"Why suddenly so shy? If I remember correctly, you assured me everything you did was quite legal."

Well, I certainly deserved that, Luz thought. Rita had sworn her caustic tongue would land her in trouble one day; besides, what else could she expect? He had found her lolling around half-naked, apparently more than willing to invite familiarity with just any male who happened along. It hadn't helped her image when she had gushed like an adoring, panting groupie about his films, either. And now

28

she was sure he had sensed the pleasure she couldn't hide when he had held her close to his body, or when he had stroked her legs. What was the matter with her suddenly —had she become demented?

"Look, Luz, let's stop playing games . . ."

She didn't blame him, not really, so there was no quick anger when she removed his arm from where it had slipped to her waist. "I think we've both made a mistake. Now I think I'd better go find Rita. I'm sorry if I wasted your evening, but I'm not very good playing your kind of games."

"That's not what I meant."

The sincerity in his voice stopped her movement toward the house. "What *did* you mean?"

"Only that I can understand how you feel about that mayhem going on in there because I find it just as stupid and brainless as you find it. Do you want to spend the rest of the night caught up in that garbage?"

"No. Oh, no!"

"Then come with me." He very deliberately kept his distance. "I don't know where I'll take you. Maybe we'll just drive somewhere for a cup of coffee, or I can take you straight home if that's what you want—but I promise to claim only a brotherly kiss on your forehead as my final reward."

The tension between them lessened, and she would have laughed outright if not for a troublesome doubt still nagging away in her brain. "What about Rita? We drove here together, and I'm sure she'll be looking for me soon."

He shrugged, but it was a gesture of compassion and not of disinterest as she had expected. "Forget her, Luz. What do you intend to do—march right in and snatch her out of Chuck's bed? All you can do as a friend is to be ready to help her when she needs you in the future. You realize that, don't you?"

He was right, of course. "Yes, I understand."

"Then come on, let's get away from this place."

Why not? It would be a blessing to leave the madness and the noise far behind. But her desire to be with him was truly the real reason why she answered, "Yes, let's go, quickly!"

This time her small feet fairly flew over the roughness of the driveway. "Mario?"

"What is it?" He moved swiftly to keep up with her dizzy pace.

"You haven't forgotten your promise, have you?"

"My promise?"

A pixieish impulse pushed her to remind him, *"No te olvidas tu promesa a besar me como un hermano más tarde esta noche."*

His laughter was as strong as the arm that reached out again to hold her. "I won't forget. Just a brotherly kiss, *te lo juro!"*

CHAPTER TWO

The drive back through the canyon floor was accomplished in mutual silence. Mario handled his sleek sports car smoothly around the devious obstacles, while Luz leaned back against the yielding lightness of the leather headrest. She was staring up at the sky; how dark it was! The wind had shifted, and it was blowing in from the desert, warm and dry.

Mario looked at Luz for a second. Circles of air were

playing havoc with her hair, and the silky strands slithered unbound across her face. "Shall I stop and put the top up?"

"Oh, no, please leave it down. The air feels so good." She veered around and took a glance behind the seat. "Besides, my shoes aren't dry yet."

The same image sprang to their minds at exactly the same time. "What a silly thing to happen," she laughed, remembering the drenching. Thank goodness her dress and hair had dried. "I don't think I'm fit to be seen in public."

"You look fine to me." His smile reassured her more than his words. "Any other woman I know would have come apart at the seams."

Luz was sure he had women by the droves. His looks and success would have attracted them like flies. Was there a special "other woman"? "What about your date? You didn't tell her you were leaving, you know."

"I'll apologize tomorrow . . . or next week . . . maybe."

So much for the abandoned receptionist! Luz settled back, thinking over the past few hours. Strangely, it was Chuck's image that stuck in her mind the most. She disliked him, she decided, remembering his swaggering machismo. The contrast between him and Mario was so obvious that she wondered aloud, "Are you and Chuck good friends?"

"We're not friends at all. We met a few months ago at the studio, but it's been strictly business, until tonight." A hard line appeared at the edge of his mouth. "Chuck is supposed to be a damned fine casting director, but now I understand why he doesn't get too much work done. It's not only the parties and the booze. He spends the rest of his time hallucinating about becoming a big-shot producer. He has his problems and I have mine. But now his problems are starting to get in my way—and I don't like that." There was a pause. "Sorry," he apologized with a smile so mesmerizing that Luz could have forgiven him anything, "but I didn't mean to bore you with shoptalk."

Luz marveled at the way Mario could compel her to confide even her innermost thoughts. "I dreaded going to Chuck's house tonight because I knew I would be buried in shoptalk." She put her head back and closed her eyes. "I don't know which I find more uninteresting, the people or their stories. But I don't find you uninteresting . . . nothing you say to me could possibly be boring."

"Do you always say exactly what you think and feel?"

The subtle change in his tone bore a hint of disapproval that startled Luz. "It's a habit I've never outgrown. Does it displease you?" she murmured, opening her eyes and turning her head toward him just a little.

Traffic was light; even so, he seemed to find it necessary to keep looking straight ahead. "It's the type of habit that can boomerang, hurting you badly, especially when you confide in somebody you don't know at all," he said, ignoring the main thrust of her question. "I don't want to see you hurt, Luz."

The warning was clear and simple: Keep things bright and impersonal! Only a complete fool could ignore his meaning, and Luz was far from being a fool. She sat up abruptly and looked at the houses, at the hills, at the lights, and at everything else passing by—but she did not look at him. They had traveled midtown and soon Sunset Boulevard would skim alongside the downtown freeway interchange, change names, and then cross over the concrete bed of the Los Angeles River. Then she would be in her own territory, in the *barrios,* where she wouldn't have to guard herself against showing emotion, where she wouldn't have to carefully scrutinize every word before speaking. The lovely bouncing lights from the Music Center's gigantic chandeliers reached her eyes. She was almost home. And then, thankfully, this strange, disturbing evening would be over. But . . . she didn't want it to end because of him, especially not like this. "It's a lucky thing you just happened to drive down this way. I live right over there in East Los Angeles." He was probably enormously relieved. She groped around the back of the car for her shoes, found them, and swiftly slipped them on. "If you just follow Sunset . . ."

"I know the way. I was born in the *barrio*. It's been a few years since I've set foot in the old neighborhood, but I think I can still find my way around."

But before they reached the old tunnel that would lead on to the bridge he turned the car suddenly, driving past the graceful grandeur of the Union Station, which still served as the city's main railroad terminal.

"Perhaps it's been *too* many years," Luz reminded him, "because this street heads south and I live across the river . . ."

"I'm not taking you home." His gaze strayed beyond Luz's surprised face, scanning for a spot to park. "All of a sudden, I'm hungry. Mind eating Mexican food, or are you bored with that, too?" he teased.

"Certainly not." For the first time it dawned on her that he had been teasing her for the better part of the evening. Ordinarily she would have been annoyed; she hated being teased. However, nothing could ever be ordinary if it involved Mario Maldonado. He parked the car with ease in a pocket-sized space, walked around to her side, and helped her climb out. Again, he gave her no opportunity to protest, and once again she found herself not minding at all. Neither did he seem to mind that she was studying him when he took off his jacket and swung it over one shoulder while opening his shirt collar with his free hand. The same copper hue of his face met her eye as her gaze slipped down from his exposed neck to the burnished smoothness of his chest. His thin white shirt barely hid the flow of muscles beneath its silky sheen, tough tight muscles that hardened even more in an involuntary reflex

33

when her small fingers curled around his back. It was a natural thing for her to place her hand there—he had brought his arm up around her shoulders, capturing her body so that it fit close to his hip. The brittle film of cautious politeness that had existed between them snapped—and she was glad to be rid of it!

They began to walk. "It's been years since I've visited la Calle Olvera, too," he said, holding back his long strides so that Luz wouldn't trip over the uneven stones of the city's oldest, most historic street, "but I also think I can remember a *puesto* that serves up the best *taquitos* in L.A."

They strolled along, her body moving in slow harmony with his body, and a sweetness that could only be night-blooming jasmine lingered in the air. They placidly shared the spectacle of the gaily painted souvenir stands and restaurants. Each *puesto,* regardless of its size, bore a legend or title proudly etched somewhere on its wooden boards. A miniature stand selling beautiful handmade pottery was called "El Rancho Grande" and farther on an equally small food stand reflected the same humor by calling itself "El Palacio."

"Here's the place." Mario grinned, finally stopping in front of a small café. Huge earthen pots simmered away right in the open window, and the aroma arising from their contents was absolutely delightful.

Luz inspected the steaming array of beans, rice, *salsas,* and fresh corn *tortillas* with an expert eye. Satisfied, she nodded. "If this food tastes anywhere as good as it smells and looks, then I have to admire your memory."

"Just wait," he promised. "The quality of the food isn't the only reason why I suddenly remembered this place. Look up there." He was pointing to the café's name. Painted with a flourish were the words "La Luz del Dia." "Now what do you think of my memory?"

"I don't know what to say . . . !"

She was saved by the cook's voice asking for their order.

Business was brisk and he was the café's only waiter, too.

"*¿Su orden, señor?*"

"*Dos ordenes de taquitos, por favor.*"

"*¿Con arroz y frijóles?*"

Mario raised a questioning eyebrow at Luz. She shook her head. "Oh, no, without rice and beans, please." Mario chose the combination plate, and they watched as the cook turned into an instant artist. His fingers flew over the pots and—presto!—two paper plates appeared heaped with culinary magic.

"*¿Para comer aquí, o se lo llevan?*" The cook nodded toward an empty table far in the rear.

Luz breathed in the jasmine-scented air. "No, let's take the food and eat it somewhere in the open."

"Fine," Mario agreed. Armed with plenty of paper napkins to catch the overflow of spicy *guacamole* sauce that was the topping glory of any *taquito,* they walked slowly to the end of the old *calle* to the plaza. The filigreed spaciousness of the *kiosco* beckoned and they settled down comfortably on one of the wide stone benches.

"What's the verdict?" he asked, after Luz had bitten into the rolled *tortilla* filled with meat.

"Wonderful!" The rest of the meal was eaten in the respectful silence it deserved. Other people milled around, some just enjoying the peacefulness of the place, some selling flowers, jewelry, or toys.

A young vendor approached Mario and coaxed, "*¡Andale, señor! ¿Una vela de perfume para su novia hermosa?*"

"*Amor,*" Mario said to Luz, not bothering to correct the youngster's mistaken assumption that they were newly-weds, "why don't you pick out a candle?"

Assuming the same casual manner, Luz chose a white candle shaped like a fragile flower. The boy scurried off quickly with Mario's generous tip stuffed deeply in his pocket. An insignificant incident, she thought, cradling the waxed blossom in her palm. But why didn't she trust herself to speak? And why had the twinkle disappeared from Mario's dark eyes?

"That kid reminds me of myself at that age." Such a simple statement, but to Luz it said much.

"He seemed like a bright, happy boy," she responded, hoping Mario would continue, and amazed her voice remained so steady.

"Bright? Well, in some ways, I guess I was. As for happy . . . yes, I was happy, sometimes." He stretched, clasped his hands behind his head, and leaned back against one of the *kiosco's* iron girders. "Smartest thing I did was to stick it out at school when most of my buddies were dropping out. I learned early that you can't get very far with only a smartass street education." His smile showed he was far away in the past. "When the community services began giving out grants in the *barrios,* I got lucky. I made my first film at nineteen. It wasn't very good, of course, but it opened doors. From then on, I've been proud of some of the work I've done." He wasn't boasting, he was only reliving experiences.

"And when you're working, is that when you're happiest?"

"How did you know that?"

Had she pulled another blunder insinuating something personal into their conversation? But he didn't look displeased; he had moved closer, resting on his arm. Her self-confidence returned and she replied with candor, "Since you hadn't mentioned your family I assumed your career means everything to you."

"A person can't describe something he's never had. Oh, I suppose I have relatives somewhere out there, but I've never known any of them." He took the candle out of her hand, set it aside, and clasped both of them within his. "But enough about me. You've tricked me into doing all the talking. What about you?" He stroked the sides of her fingers lightly and gently, back and forth. "Can I assume a few things about you, too?"

"Such as what?" The caressing movements of his fingertips were igniting currents of pleasure along her arms. She prayed he wouldn't stop.

"You weren't born here in L.A.—your Spanish was learned in Mexico, not stateside. And I would say you come from a large happy family, that you have lots of brothers and sisters, that you have one hell of a mind in that beautiful head of yours, *and* that you always get what you want." He bent his head and touched her palm lightly with his lips. "How did I do?"

"Not bad." Did he always carry on a casual conversation like this? "My family is small, but happy. I have only a sister and a brother and they're both much older than I am." She deliberately did not comment on the rest of his conclusions.

"No parents?"

"They were killed in a bus accident when I was a child. We had lived on a ranch in Jalisco, not a big ranch, but it was good and we were happy. After the accident, only my brother was left to take care of me because my sister had come to live in Los Angeles." She faltered, feeling the old searing sadness.

"Go on," he urged softly. His hold on her hands was compassionate now.

"My brother had just begun to study in the seminary and couldn't possibly deal with an energetic ten-year-old tomboy, so I was sent here to be brought up by my sister, Trina. She's been more like my mother, really, and I love her very much. And Rita has been like a sister. I don't think I will ever again be as unhappy and as frightened as I was the day I arrived in this city. But, since then, I too have been happy . . . sometimes."

Startled, she found that her head had fallen upon his shoulder. How many minutes passed after she had stopped speaking? The plaza was almost deserted. Bits of papers drifted by, flying on a breeze that had turned chilly. She shuddered even though Mario's arms were holding her. His lips brushed against her forehead. "Now you've used up your promise to kiss me good night like a brother."

"I would have broken that promise, anyway," he murmured.

"It's late." She reluctantly withdrew out of his arms. "I must really be getting home."

He walked with her through the front yard gate. Not big enough to be called a garden, the small yard nevertheless bloomed with azaleas and cactus-roses. The modest white house looked comfortably settled on its grounds although no welcoming lights shone either inside or out. The neighboring houses up and down the quiet residential street almost exactly resembled the Rivas household except for individual touches of color. All in all, totally middle class, and slightly different from the part of the *barrio* where Mario had grown up.

"I'd like to ask you to come in for that cup of coffee, but I'm afraid my sister has gone to sleep and I wouldn't want to wake her."

Mario read the luminous dial on his wristwatch. "I didn't think it was that late."

"Oh, Trina has been asleep for hours. She gets up at four o'clock every morning," Luz said, stopping automatically at the bottom of the small bank of steps she knew led to the front door.

"My God! Four in the *morning?*"

"That's right. First she goes to Mass . . ."

"Every morning?"

"Yes, every morning. Then she hurries to open *la panaderia* . . ."

"She works in a bakery?"

"No, she *owns* the bakery," Luz laughed. "I was always

the envy of all my schoolmates at the convent because every day I would have a luscious, fresh piece of cake in my lunchbox. Now I take a large carton of cakes to the studio at least once a week for everybody to enjoy at coffee break."

"Tell you what," he said wistfully. "You bring with you one of those round *pan de huevo*—the kind with the cinnamon sugar on top—and I'll buy you a gallon of coffee!" The frivolous timbre in his voice fell away without warning. "Don't worry if you forget, Luz. Then I'll have a damned good excuse to call you."

Earlier, when they had left Olvera Street, he had put his jacket around her shoulders because of the sudden coldness of the summer fog. She still wore it. Now she lifted the warm jacket away and returned it to him. Another step brought her closer to him, and then the narrow space separating them disappeared.

"You don't need an excuse to call me, Mario," she whispered. She grazed her mouth against his for a moment; the beguiling male scent of his hair, skin, and breath rushed at her. His taut palms tightened on the back of her neck and squeezed her forward, bringing their already parted lips together. He slowly shifted his mouth so it would envelop the soft mound of her mouth, and then she felt his tongue stab into her, exploring all the warm, moist secrets inside. And while his kiss was scalding her deep and hot, he very gradually, very arousingly let his hands move over her face, her throat, and then her back, firing the lovely flesh beneath into a mass of flames. For a long time they stood molded together, swaying, suspended between the slender limit of discovery and real desire. Inevitably, uncontrollably, his hand swept forward to seek the downy curve of her breast, and his fingers spontaneously convulsed when he encountered the small puckered spot in its center.

She threw her head back. "Yes," she moaned. Then, "No, I . . ."

"Don't . . ."

"Not here, not like this!"

Then he murmured words that fed her excitement in spite of their desperate breathlessness, and she appeased a tiny part of her quickening hunger by tasting his mouth again. They remained so intensely linked together that they heard nothing and knew nothing but each other.

It was the snarling sound and not the cruel shaft of light that finally wedged them apart. *"Luz!"*

But for Mario's arm still holding onto her waist Luz would have stumbled as she twirled around. "What on earth are you doing out of bed, Trina?"

There was no answer from the woman who stood rigidly silhouetted in the doorway, but every inch of her body seemed to be rent with a terrible anger.

"I'm sorry we woke you—go back to sleep—I'll come into the house in a few minutes, all right?" Luz continued. The tremor in her voice clearly betrayed the fact that she was shocked and surprised by her sister's strange behavior. She felt Mario's hand slip encouragingly around her own hand.

"No! Not in a few minutes! I want you in this house *immediately!"* A second later Trina Rivas was gone from the doorway, but the door remained open, flooding the yard with light. From deep within the house a door banged like a shot.

Luz looked at Mario, her eyes clearly showing her amazement. "I don't understand what's gotten into her!" She tried a smile, but was a total failure. "She's never acted like this before!"

"Luz, would it help if I stayed and . . . ?"

"I don't know what to think. No, thank you. I'd better go inside and try to calm her down."

"You're sure now?"

"Yes."

"Okay, you know best." He gently brushed her lips with his fingers, and a second later he was gone. Luz waited until she couldn't hear the sound of his car anymore. Still nerved up by Mario's caresses and shaken by her own response, she climbed the steps and entered the house.

Why wouldn't the words stop jumping around all over the page this morning? Luz realized her hands were trembling as she held the manuscript. She also realized she had read the same sentence for the tenth time. Giving up, she slammed the script down on her desk.

Betsy Luger looked up, surprised. "The script's that bad, huh?"

Betsy was Luz's assistant and they shared the same office, an arrangement that sometimes grated on Luz's nerves. And this morning was definitely one of those times, especially since Betsy persisted, "I've told you a million times . . . why don't you write your own script!"

Luz rubbed her tired eyes, then forced herself to smile over at the unattractive girl. "You know, Betsy, I just might one of these days." It was an idea that had been growing in her mind lately. She was sure she could come up with something better than many of the stories that crossed her desk every day. The main problem was finding an interesting theme, something that would appeal both to the public and to herself.

"You're not expecting an important phone call, are you?" asked Betsy, staring at Luz through her large, bug-eyed glasses. On anyone else the fashionable glasses would have looked interesting, at least, but on Betsy, along with anything else she wore, they just somehow looked weird. Betsy was shapeless, dumpy, and man-hungry. Also desperate. Her thirtieth birthday had come and gone . . . two years ago. "You've been staring at that phone all morning!"

So she had. Would she ever see him again, she wondered, after what had happened last night? She covered her eyes, banishing the scene away. Of all the embarrassing, idiotic things to happen!

"Hey, are you feeling okay?"

"Sure, I'm fine. I didn't get much sleep last night, that's all." Now *that* was the understatement of the year. "Why don't you let me get you a cup of coffee?" Anything to get away from Betsy's constant prattle—anything to stop thinking about Mario, and about why he hadn't called yet.

Luz was out of the office before Betsy could say "no." She walked just as quickly along the corridors, hoping no one would stop and talk to her. The business offices of Mercury Studios were hardly a beehive of activity at this late hour of the morning. Sometimes bedlam abounded, but today everything was muffled and quiet. The smoked glass doors of the executive suites were shut. Only the stark faces of African sculptures and unreal Dada-like paintings looked down upon Luz from the beige walls. All the decor was dark wood and chromium, and she rather liked it, but today all the darkness only depressed her. She hurriedly entered the small room set aside for coffee and refreshments, and busied herself for a second setting the correct buttons for the brew—one black for herself, one with extra cream and sugar for Betsy. The machine efficiently took care of everything and the coffee was ready in twenty seconds. She hesitated. Alone for the first time in hours, she leaned her forehead against the cool wood paneling and let all the pent-up frustration break through. She had been unable to find out what had triggered Trina's outburst last night; when she had knocked on her sister's bedroom door there had been nothing but silence. Trina had quietly and swiftly left the house by the time Luz had finally staggered out of bed this morning after a hellish, sleepless night of twisting and turning. Luz could make no sense whatsoever out of the puzzle. Trina had always been more than tolerant, even when she had found Luz necking and petting just a little with high school Romeos. Perhaps something else was bothering Trina, perhaps she was sick . . .

Pulling herself together, Luz picked up the coffee cups and left the room, remembering something else. Mario had said he would call, but he hadn't specifically said he would call her *today*, had he? Walking back to her office she promised herself to stop daydreaming and acting like a teenager mooning over her first kiss! The whole thing was becoming ridiculous, anyway. She felt much better— until she passed Chuck Harrison's office. The door was shut; obviously no one was in there. And Rita? What had happened to Rita?

She found out the moment she stepped into her office. Rita was perched comfortably in Luz's chair looking fresh and lovely, dressed in an expensive high-fashion set of white fishnet top and pants, chatting with Betsy.

"Hi, Luz! Sorry I didn't pick you up this morning." They usually car pooled and this was Rita's week to drive. "I had a few things to do so I left the house early."

Which house, wondered Luz? Her mother's house, or Chuck's? And where was Chuck—still languishing asleep in bed? But she only replied, "That's okay, Rita." Luz handed Betsy her coffee, and turned to look at Rita again. A tense, wordless antagonism seemed to erupt between the two women. Luz waited, sipping her coffee.

"By the way, how did you get home last night?" Rita tried to keep her keen interest out of her voice. "I looked all over for you—so did Chuck—but you had disappeared."

Luz noticed out of the corner of her eye that Betsy suddenly was very involved in her typing, but her ears were definitely cocked to catch every word Luz and Rita were saying. "Actually, I left rather early."

"I don't know why," Rita snapped back. "Everybody

else was enjoying the party." She waited a second before attacking again. "But you haven't told me . . . how did you get home?"

"I'm sure the name means nothing to you, but Mario Maldonado drove me home."

If Luz had ignited a small bomb in the room the results could not have been more spectacular. Rita's mouth gaped open, but it was Betsy who squeaked incredulously, "You left the party with *Mario Maldonado?*"

"That's right. Why so surprised?" She felt suddenly ambushed from both sides. To cover up her nervousness, she inquired rather sarcastically, "If our conversation is interfering with your work, Betsy . . . ?"

Betsy jumped up from her chair and dashed around the desk. "The heck with my work! Tell us about Mario Maldonado!"

Luz was really stunned. "What's so extraordinary about the fact that Mario drove me home? What's the matter with you two, anyway?"

Rita finally recovered the full use of her tongue. "You're really something else, Luz Rivas, you know that? You sit up here in your little office, working earnestly, pure and innocent—and yet you somehow manage to snare the sexiest prize package of the year."

"Well, yes, I agree he's very good-looking . . ."

"Good-looking!" hooted Betsy. "Is that all you noticed about him? Don't you know that every female between puberty and senility has been killing herself to make any kind of an impression on that lovely, lovely man since he started working here at Mercury?"

"He's working on a film, *here,* at this studio?" So that's what he was beginning to talk about last night in the car.

"They haven't started shooting the film yet, but he's been here for a number of conferences, especially with Chuck." Rita sounded a little defensive, and Luz wondered about that. Then she remembered Mario had mentioned Chuck's working habits with less than heartfelt praise, and a number of details about last night's conversation suddenly made sense. "Funny how things work in circles," Rita went on a little too flippantly. "Chuck wants you to come with me tonight to look over a possible 'new face' for Mario's' film." She bit her lip thoughtfully. "Chuck's had a lot of trouble finding just the right person for this part, and Maldonado is getting a little testy about the delay."

"Why doesn't Chuck go and look for himself?"

"He can't."

Luz didn't like the way Rita giggled. Whenever Rita giggled like that lately it always meant trouble. "Okay, I'll bite. Why can't he?"

"Because the part calls for a young, sexy Chicano type —and this young, sexy Chicano works in a for-women-only club. He's a disco dancer at Roxie's!"

"Fabulous place," interrupted Betsy. "I've been there, and it's a great place to check out some terrific guys."

"Why does Chuck want *me* to go with you to that place, anyway?"

"He values your opinion. You impressed him with your mind last night." Rita deliberately made the remark sound like an insult. "Come on, Luz," she coaxed like a vixen, "if you won't do it for Chuck, at least do it for Mario Maldonado. I don't know what *went on* between you and Mario last night, but you don't want him all upset and frustrated, do you? He insists Chuck find a real Latino to play the part and not just somebody who looks Mexican," she pouted, "and Chuck says he has quite a temper."

Luz saw both women staring at her as if she were a specimen under a microscope. She relented, but not for the reasons Rita had suggested. "All right, I'll go to Roxie's with you, but only to help you out, Rita."

"Thanks," Rita answered, but she stared down at the floor.

Betsy's loud voice broke into the awkward moment. "I think one of the reasons why he's so exotic is because Mario Maldonado is one of the first Mexican-Americans to break into the film business." Getting blank looks from both Luz and Rita, she continued undaunted, "Well, you know what I mean. He's refreshingly different!"

Rita laughed, but Luz couldn't help reminding her, "Oh, I thought he interested you only because he was generally sensual and sexy?"

"Of course. Those are the most important reasons." Betsy didn't believe in being subtle.

"Luz, I have to run," Rita broke in before Luz could say anything. "I'll pick you up after dinner at home?"

"Yes." She remembered Trina. She had to have time to talk to her sister. "Yes, but make it about an hour after dinner, okay?"

"Sure." Rita waved good-bye and rushed out.

Feeling drained, knowing she would get to bed late again tonight, Luz sat down and closed her eyes.

"Why don't you knock it off early and go home?" Betsy suggested, a note of real concern in her voice. "I can hold down the fort here."

"I think I will." Luz stretched and took a deep breath. She smiled at Betsy. "Thanks."

"Don't mention it," she replied with a wicked wink.

Luz laughed for the first time that day.

She noticed the enticing aroma of something special cooking the moment she entered the house. Although it would be at least an hour until dinner time, Luz knew she would find Trina in the kitchen.

"Ah, Luz, I'm glad you're home early. Please set the table for me, won't you?" Trina beamed and gave Luz her usual kiss. She bustled about the kitchen, matronly and motherly, humming all the while. It was as if the incident last night had never happened.

46

"Yes, of course." Luz was puzzled. "Trina, I'm sorry we woke you last night. If I had known you were not asleep, we would have come into the house right away. I really wanted you to meet . . ."

Trina's eyes quickly narrowed, and she shook her head, clearly warning Luz to stop talking. Speaking much louder than necessary, she instructed Luz to set the table for three tonight, ". . . and please put out the good china, won't you?"

So they were having a guest for dinner; no wonder Trina had not wished to discuss family matters. But why all the exaggerated secrecy? Whoever it was must be sitting within earshot in the living room.

Luz kept her voice down. "Who is joining us for dinner?"

"It's a surprise." Trina smiled vaguely, stirring up a storm at the stove.

But Luz was tired and she didn't want any surprises. "Who is it," she insisted.

Trina laid the big cooking spoon aside and turned around, wearing the same expression she had used when she wanted Luz to behave when she was a child. "Jorge Garcia."

"Jorge . . . !" Luz almost stuttered in amazement. "When did he arrive in Los Angeles?"

"Sh-h-h, keep your voice down! He arrived yesterday. He phoned last night, of course, but you weren't home, *if you remember*. I had just gotten home from the movies when the phone began ringing. He said he had been calling all night. Where did you go last night?"

"I went to a party with Rita." The moment she spoke the words she was sorry.

"So." Trina's large brown eyes filled with worry and she looked much, much older than her years. Luz's heart constricted at the sight. Her sister was only ten years older, but she appeared to be an old woman. Life had been

47

hard for Trina Rivas since she had chosen to leave her family and begin a new life in Los Angeles. But she had worked hard, first as an employee at the bakery, and then as the owner of the same establishment. She had put a small down payment on this house after years of saving every penny she earned, and now the mortgage was almost paid, thanks to Luz's help. The years of toil and the added responsibility of taking care of Luz during the most difficult years of the youngster's life had badly taken its toll. However, although now she was living a more comfortable, secure life, Trina still worried about Luz. And about Rita, too. Hadn't she known the Campos girl since babyhood? Her eyes moist, Trina stirred the pots and continued her lament. "Mrs. Campos called me today, weeping. Rita didn't come home last night—again. That girl has turned into a little tramp! Such a pity. She comes from such a nice family." Trina's mouth turned down in sorrow. "Did Rita introduce you to that man you were kissing last night?"

"No." She didn't want to explain anything about Mario. Anyway, what could she honestly say? "Look, I love you very much, but you've wasted your time asking Jorge to come here again." She turned away before Trina could come back at her with the same old argument. "Oh, don't worry. I'll set the table and say hello to our honored guest like a properly brought up young lady."

Now Luz understood everything. *Jorge Garcia, for God's sake!* She set the table with extra care because deep down inside she really wanted to smash every dish on the floor. Jorge had first come to ask for her hand in marriage on her eighteenth birthday. A widower with grown children, he was a "close friend of the family" and came every year without fail to ask her to marry him. Luz knew that Jorge was ably supported on his useless yearly missions by letters from her sister, who was only concerned that Luz should "make a good marriage with a good man," and by

Luz's brother, who was the parish priest in the area of Jalisco where Jorge owned a rather large cattle ranch. Now here he was again, still hoping to talk her into marriage. No wonder Trina had been so upset when she had seen Mario last night, especially because her little baby sister must have appeared more than willing to find herself tightly clutched in his arms!

She put the last plate in place, straightened her shoulders like a soldier going into battle, and walked into the living room. Jorge Garcia sat comfortably on the sofa drinking a Jerez. He stood up quite formally the minute Luz entered the room. "Ah, Luz, how are you?"

"Very well, Jorge, thank you." The rituals and traditions had to be followed to the letter, even in conversation. She bent her head for his very correct kiss on the forehead.

"Your brother, who is a true servant of God, sends his love and his blessings."

"Please tell my brother when you return to Mexico that I shall always cherish his affection."

With that part of the formal greeting out of the way, Jorge led Luz to a chair. She sat, carefully tucked her skirt modestly around her knees, and then watched Jorge regain his place on the sofa. He was not aging well. He had a paunch and his hair was thinning. He spent most of his time outdoors and the sun had stained his skin a deep ruddy red. Luz had always disliked him, and she wondered why he just didn't give up and marry some nice girl back home.

"I will give your brother your message. But, Luz, I had hoped that *this* time you could tell him of your affection and *obedience* yourself."

Luz did not miss the fine point of that remark. "Then I would only have to add the same thing I've been telling you for eight years now, Jorge. I cannot marry you."

Trina would have to come in at just that moment! She gave Luz a reprimanding glance and announced that dinner was ready to be served. Jorge led Trina to the dining room and stood behind her chair until she was seated. Luz was assigned the proper role as the younger female member of the family . . . she served the dinner. That done, she could be seated.

Conversation proceeded at a leisurely pace, mostly tidbits about mutual friends both here and in Mexico. Jorge went into a long monologue about his ranch, his wealth, and the new house he was planning on building. "If only you would grace it with your presence, Luz. I know you would be happy, and you could make me so happy." He did not give Luz a chance to reply to that remark, and the dinner dragged on and on. Trina had prepared a huge meal centered around turkey basted in *mole,* which was a very heavy sauce made from red chili, cinnamon, and chocolate. Each bite fell in Luz's stomach like lead. After only two or three attempts, she finally pushed her plate away. Sooner or later she would have to tell Trina that she was going out with Rita again tonight.

"Luz, you are not eating," Trina noted.

"I'm not hungry. Sorry."

"You are very tired, and that's why you're not hungry. You should get to sleep at nights, and stop all this running around."

For some reason, this remark seemed to interest Jorge. "What do you mean?" he asked, addressing Trina, but looking at Luz.

"Wild friends, you know," Trina nodded to Jorge, meaningfully.

"Ah, I see," Jorge muttered, understanding all the wrong things from that remark. He again looked over at Luz; there was a marked change in his appraisal, but neither woman noticed.

Luz thought she might as well get it over with. "I'll be going out again tonight, I'm afraid, so I will have to leave you soon. Rita and I have to do some work for a new film at the studio." There was no use going into the real details. Trina would probably have a stroke. "Shall I clear the table now?"

"No," Trina replied, looking very annoyed, "you entertain Jorge in the living room and I shall take care of the table."

Luz groaned inwardly. Now she would have to listen to Jorge reaffirm his "intentions," then he would ask her to marry him again, then she would decline his proposal, and then Trina would spend another year urging her to change her mind. The whole damned thing was stupid. But she played the charade for yet another time. For Trina's sake, and for her brother's. Only this time, there was a difference in Jorge's approach . . .

She had just finished politely saying "no" again, and she wasn't really paying much attention to what he was saying because she was straining to hear the sound of Rita's car. The only thing she could hear, however, was the sound of Trina rattling pots and dishes in the kitchen. Oh, why didn't Rita hurry up! Suddenly, she realized Jorge had stopped talking. He was sitting next to her, and he was sitting very close. "Your sister does not understand that young people today have different values, different ways of looking at life. I understand, however. Wild friends, eh? Well, I don't mind, Luz."

He had a dull gleam in his eye that Luz didn't quite like. He had digested Trina's remark and had drawn his own dirty conclusions, obviously. She suppressed an urge to laugh right in his face.

"Do you ever wonder why I keep coming back here, hoping you will marry me?" he asked in a funny, low growl.

"Frankly, yes. Why don't you find somebody else to marry?" She moved away slightly.

"Because I've been thinking only of you since the first

51

time I saw you." There was no mistaking his ardor this time.

"Jorge, I don't think . . ."

"I dream of you." His arm clutched her around the waist, and he lunged at her.

She parried his embrace and thrust herself toward the end of the sofa, which was the wrong thing to do because now he had her cornered.

"Jorge, stop! My sister . . ."

"Don't worry, she trusts me. She would even trust me if we were *alone* in this house. Would you like that, Luz?" He sought her mouth roughly. "You think I'm old—but I'm not. Let me show you . . . !"

She wrenched her face to the side, desperately avoiding his wet lips. "You let me go!" What might have seemed somewhat funny at the start was turning into an ugly wrestling match. She didn't dare raise her voice, but every second brought more of his heavy weight bearing down on her and she was sickeningly revolted.

"Kiss me, kiss me only once . . . !" Straining to reach her mouth and failing, he began to chew hard and noisily at her neck.

She could hardly breathe. But when he poked one heavy paw under her dress, she gasped so violently that he relaxed his hold for a split second. She flung herself from his disgusting embrace and jumped from the sofa. Bringing her hands tightly over her lips to silence any further gasps, she stood rooted in the center of the room. If he lunged at her again, she was determined to scream as loudly as she possibly could. He watched her like a hunter sighting his prey, pale under his scorched skin and sweating like a beast himself.

When Rita's voice reached her ears, it was as welcome as a blast of cold clean air. Their words mingling together, Trina and Rita were greeting each other stiffly, but to Luz it was the sweetest sound in the world. Still shaking, she smoothed her hair back and straightened her dress. Jorge had taken out a large handkerchief and was swabbing away at his face and neck. Luz knew both women would be coming into the room in a second, so she backed farther away but hissed clearly enough for him to hear, "I want you to go away and *never come back,* do you understand?"

When Rita appeared at the door with Trina close behind, everything looked perfectly normal. Jorge was pouring himself another drink and Luz was managing a light smile. *Thank God* Trina was oblivious to what had just taken place, but Rita's glance darted from Luz to Jorge and she swiftly got the picture.

"Are you ready, Luz?" Rita smiled blandly over at Jorge. "Good evening, Mr. Garcia." She knew the whole story concerning his eight-year quest to marry Luz. "When will you be returning to Mexico?"

Trina sniffed at Rita's rudeness. What else could be expected from such a wild, immoral girl?

"Tomorrow." Jorge Garcia was having trouble speaking clearly.

"Then I'll say good-bye now," Luz said in a rush, running to stand by Rita. "Have a good trip back, Jorge."

"Thank you" was his only reply.

Luz gave her sister a hug and ignored the disappointment in the tired brown eyes. "Please get to bed early," she pleaded, "and don't wait up for me tonight. Promise, Trina?"

Her sister reluctantly nodded. Another year lost! Another year of worry and fear while Luz was being influenced by Rita!

Luz practically pulled Rita out of the house. Once in Rita's car, Luz laughed for the second time that day— only this time she couldn't stop laughing.

CHAPTER THREE

"You mean that fat old goat actually got all steamed up, right there in your sister's living room?"

"Oh, Rita, it would have been hilarious, only I was so worried that Trina would hear everything!"

"Why should you care?" Rita laughed, paying little attention to her driving. The car hurtled forward, crossing three lanes of the freeway in one wild dash. "It's about time your goody-goody sister learned that Mr. Jorge 'Purity' Garcia wants to drag you off to that one-horse *pueblo* in Mexico for more than just fetching water from the stream. Doesn't she know that lust and sex exist?"

"Don't joke about it, Rita. It was pretty disgusting. Anyway, Trina and I have never discussed sex," Luz said. "I can't honestly ever remember hearing her say the word."

"But she doesn't mind discussing other topics that she also doesn't know a thing about, right?" Rita had stopped laughing. "She's been burning up the phone wires between her house and mine."

"Your mother called my sister, not the other way around. Your mom was upset because you didn't come home last night."

"And then you wonder why I want to get out of that house?" Rita cried. She drove her foot down harder on the accelerator.

54

"For God's sake, you'll kill us in this traffic if you don't slow down!"

"Okay, don't get excited." Rita took a deep breath and eased the pressure off the pedal. "I know your family doesn't approve of me anymore." There was a poignant sob in her voice, but she said nothing else and drove more slowly.

They left the freeway and turned west on Sunset Boulevard toward the Strip. Block after block of sleazy shops and motels unfolded. A kid stood on the corner of Sunset and La Brea selling maps to movie stars' homes. But soon the appearance of the boulevard changed and improved. They were rounding the looping curves of the Strip, and they had traveled to another world. Flashing billboards touting super rock and punk groups towered above chic boutiques and outdoor cafés that served only organically grown food. Everything was ablaze with lights. Rita pulled into the far left lane and turned down a steep street.

"I hope Juanito Jimenez turns out to be as hunky in person as he appears in his pictures," Rita grunted, pushing down hard on the brakes with all her strength.

"So that's the name of the kid we're going to see," Luz said. "Do you know anything about him?"

"Yeah, one or two things. Comes from right out of the *barrio,* attended Lincoln High but dropped out, and is one heck of a dancer."

"How old is he?"

"Young—but he's been around!"

The neon sign ahead loudly proclaimed "Roxie's." Like so many discos and restaurants in West Hollywood, the club was really two large California bungalows stuck together with a false front. Flashing thunderbolts of blue neon surrounded life-sized pictures of six members of the cast performing within—all men and all young, of course. The car was handed over to the valet service, and Luz took a good look at the types of women that frequented this kind of club. Some were professional women out for a one-time lark. There were tourists, too, who were easy to spot from the native variety because most actually wore smart little hats. There were secretaries and housewives, and they came in all sizes and shapes. Clothes ranged from the "haute" to the funky . . . dresses, pants, and even shorts. One detail did surprise Luz. The male-stalking, "single" type like Betsy seemed to be in the minority; most of the women wore wedding bands.

Luz followed Rita into the main portion of the club beyond the Barbary Coast turn-of-the-century bar and she was immediately plunged into a hothouse of greenery and stained glass. As her eyes cleared in the semidarkness, she was led to a ringside table prearranged by the studio. The atmosphere was deliberately intimate and steamy; the female audience buzzed and whispered with a distinct touch of breathless self-consciousness.

Their waitress informed Luz and Rita they would be charged for two drinks apiece so they might as well order right now.

"I'll have a club soda and lime," Luz said. Tired and sleepy, she had decided not to drink tonight.

"Bring me her four drinks," Rita ordered. "It's a sin to let good alchohol go to waste."

The waitress left and Luz asked, "What exactly should we be looking for in this Juanito Jimenez—outside of the obvious, of course."

"I don't know. Chuck threw words around like 'electricity' and 'magnetic' and, well, you know."

Luz sighed and picked up the printed program. Juanito was billed as "Roxie's Macho Man" and she smiled over the blatant cliché. The waitress came swinging right back with all five drinks at one time. Rita took a swallow and peered at Luz over the top of the glass. "Didn't Mario talk about his new film last night?"

"Not much." That was true, at least. There was no use telling Rita about Mario's feelings toward Chuck.

"Ah, I see. You and Mario Maldonado were busy with other things." Rita took a smaller sip this time, licking the frost off the glass with the tip of her pointed little tongue. "Well?"

"Well—what?"

"Come on, Luz, *give!* Remember all that goop you handed me last night about being good friends and sharing everything? So? Now *you* tell *me*. The exotic Mr. Maldonado—is it all hype—or does he really deliver?"

Luz's slow flush was not caused by Rita's blunt question; it was a reaction set off by the swift, thrusting memory of Mario's strong mouth tracing a moist pattern along her throat, and his hands stroking and cajoling her flesh until it betrayed itself . . .

Rita glanced at Luz's glazed eyes, and shook her head. "Don't bother to answer. I can see the truth in your face. That good, huh?"

Canned background disco music began to blast down from the ceiling speakers, giving Luz the perfect excuse to keep silent. At the same time a blinding series of bulbs started pulsating around the curve of the stage. The music got louder and louder, the lights flashed brighter still, and in the center of it all—Juanito Jimenez burst out onto the stage.

He was the very image of "electricity" and male magnetism. Clad in a metallic black jumpsuit that fit over his rippling muscles like a second skin, striding forward provocatively, arrogantly sure of his youthful virility, he accepted the applause and whistles greeting his entrance and rewarded the women with a stunning smile. By some trick of the lighting his eyes seemed to sparkle when he smiled, but there was just a hint of cruelty about it. He wore his hair long, letting it fall below his earlobes in natural jet-black waves, and his brown skin shone under the glare of the lights. In perfect sync with the beat of the music he began to move his body and his performance was calculated to be as dramatic as it was suggestive. Using the age-old but always effective gimmick of picking out a member of the audience to involve in his routine, Juanito's eyes fell on Luz. Looking directly at her with a contrived, passionate expression, he danced closer and closer to her. Luz, suddenly in the limelight, willed herself to join in the fun and smiled right back at him. He was a great dancer, and his personality grabbed and pulled across the footlights with force. Because she was actually enjoying the act, Luz failed to see the cold mask that was falling over Rita's face; and finally, with a crash, the music stopped and the dance was over. Juanito's handsome face acknowledged the wild applause with a boyish grin. He blew Luz a kiss and then vanished through the backstage curtain as the house lights came full up.

"Well, that was a surprise. He was great!" Luz shouted over to Rita while still applauding. The tumult finally faded away and talking was easier. "Now the question is, can he act and can he speak lines?"

"With that body and that face, does it make any difference?" Rita reached over for another of the glasses. *"Wow!"*

"Don't you think you've had enough to drink? We're really here on business, you know."

Rita gulped down another swallow. "Right! Business before pleasure." She dug into her purse and found one of Chuck's executive cards. Writing a message on the back she called the waitress over. "Will you give this to Juanito Jimenez, please?"

The weary waitress rolled her eyes. "Should I put your name on the list, or do you just want to take a chance and call back next month?" She started to walk away.

"Wait a minute," Luz called to her, taking the card away from Rita. "This really is business. We're from Mercury Studios." She took a bill from her wallet and pressed it into the waitress's hand. "Please see what you can do." The waitress didn't even smile, but she hurried off.

Rita took another sip and kept her temper down. "I forgot to tell you. When we leave here, we're heading for the studio to give Chuck a firsthand report. The poor darling's working late tonight."

"Can't you phone him, Rita? I'm so tired, and I just want to get home after this."

"No, I can't phone him," Rita mimicked, starting to show the results of the alcohol. "The casting of this film has to be perfect because it's high budget. If it's a success, it can mean a lot to Chuck professionally." She suddenly became morose. "Maybe it might mean a lot to me, too."

Would it? Luz wondered. What would happen to Rita's and Chuck's relationship then? Was Rita fooling herself into thinking Chuck would marry her? But Rita was getting in a nasty mood, and Luz didn't wish to start a quarrel. She was actually relieved when she looked up and saw Juanito Jimenez.

He walked with easy strides. The black jumpsuit had been replaced by tight jeans and a gold T-shirt with "U.S. Marines" written across his bulging chest. He looked younger offstage, but he also looked confident and commanding. He was in complete control of himself, Luz realized, and if he could project that quality in his screen test, she knew he would get the part. Numerous women stopped him and talked to him. He answered casually and said funny things, and everything was very charming and easy in a teasing sort of way.

"*Hola, comadres,*" he smiled, grabbing a chair away from another table and straddling it. "What are you two Chicanas doing in this part of town," he asked, directing his eyes up around the expensive decor and indicating beyond, to the expensive locale of this establishment, "slumming?" Chuck's card dangled from his fingers.

Rita dug into her reserves, gave him one of woman-to-man looks, and missed the point in his dark humor completely. "You call this slumming? I think it's very exciting. I think your dancing was exciting, too. Would you like a drink?"

"Thanks for the compliment, but *no* to your offer. I don't drink when I'm working." He looked at Rita very deliberately, flicking the card up and down. "This card tells me you're working also."

"That's right," Rita beamed, ignoring the barb. "We're from Mercury Studios, just as the card says." She moved closer to him.

"Mercury, eh? That's the high-rent district."

"It certainly is. We came to watch you dance because the studio is interested in casting you in a film. The part's small, but whoever gets it might go on to something bigger. Sound nice?"

"Very nice." He had received offers before, and he knew how to be cautious. Most were fakes.

"I'm Rita Campos and she's Luz Rivas. I—we both think you should test for the part. Can you be at the studio tomorrow at eleven o'clock for an interview with Chuck Harrison, the casting director?"

"You bet I can."

"Beautiful." Rita touched his wrist with a little circular motion. "I'm Chuck's secretary, his private secretary, so I'll be there, too."

He merely raised his eyebrow. "That's so?" It was direct, cold, and brutal. Then he turned to Luz. "Will you be there, too, Luz?"

"No, I work in the script department."

"How about if I come around tomorrow after the interview, and we grab some lunch together?"

Luz could feel Rita's jealousy throbbing right across the table. "I almost never go out to lunch, Juanito . . ."

"No sweat, we'll talk through your lunch break, okay?"

"Okay." What else could she say? She looked at Rita and saw a vicious, violent anger in her eyes.

"I do another show later on. Why don't you stick around and the *two* of us can have that drink when I'm through?"

"I really can't, I'm sorry."

Rita laughed jeeringly. "It's way past her bedtime and she prefers to get to bed early—and alone."

She had left the implication hanging in the air, but Juanito didn't bite. "So long. I have a few other people to talk to." He grinned at Luz. "And I'll see you tomorrow, right?"

"Yes," Luz nodded, "and good luck at the interview."

Juanito sauntered away saying "Thanks again" over his shoulder.

Even in the semidarkness, Luz saw the seething, uncontrolled fury written all over Rita's face. Luz braced herself. Just as Rita had torn her dress before Chuck's party with white-hot violence, that's exactly how she looked now!

Rita stood up, none too steady on her feet. She made a dash for the door and Luz ran after her. Outside, Rita stood frozen against a wall, and Luz had to look for the parking ticket in Rita's purse. "What's the matter, Rita? Why are you so angry with me?"

Nothing, not even a word. When the car arrived, Luz pushed Rita into the passenger's seat and got behind the wheel herself.

Once out in traffic, driving was tough. The Strip was jammed with cars in both directions and a summer crowd of natives and tourists crisscrossed the streets like maniacs. At the height of the traffic snarl, Rita suddenly came to life. "You—bitch!"

Luz's first instinct was to jump out of the car, leaving Rita flat alone to fend for herself in this pandemonium.

"Don't you dare call me that!" A coldness throughout her bones kept her in her seat.

"You're a bitch and a tease! Oh, you played up to Juanito so nice and cute. Is that how you manipulated Mario? I bet you teased him the same way, but that's *all* you did. If I know you, you'll leave Juanito high and dry, too! What are you trying to do, win the prize as the biggest tease in Hollywood?" Her mouth was curled into a cruel, furious scowl, and she was so agitated that she wound her fingers around a heavy gold chain at her neck and pulled until it broke.

"If you don't shut up, I'm going to slap you right in the mouth!" Luz threatened. She meant it, and Rita suddenly realized she meant it. But the outburst seemed to clear Rita's brain and she only shrank to the side of the car, closing her eyes and pressing her head against the window.

"I'm taking you straight home. You've had too much to drink and you're going to get sick." Luz had controlled her anger and was thinking clearly now. If only this traffic would let her out of here!

"No." It came out in a dead monotone. "Go to the studio. I promised Chuck."

At last a small break in the traffic allowed Luz to turn off the Strip, and she headed toward Mercury, which was not too far away. Fine! She would drive to the studio, take Rita up to Chuck's office, and then she would grab a cab home even if it cost a fortune. She had taken enough abuse from her so-called friend.

They drove along in dead silence and soon arrived at the modern complex. "Thanks," whispered Rita, walking slowly but on a straight line to the elevators. They waited wordlessly while a car descended, then they stepped in, and Luz pushed the button that sent them shooting right up to the studio's private floor.

All the lights were on and people scurried around working on different projects. The night had been turned topsy-turvy into day. Luz had gotten used to the crazy hours in this business, and she took the no-work-day–all-work-night syndrome in stride now.

Rita walked into Chuck's office without knocking. Wondering if she should escape home without even talking to Chuck, Luz waited. No, that would be childish, she told herself, and finally entered the office.

Chuck was bent back in his tilted executive chair with his feet propped up on the desk, and Rita hovered at his side, but she was staring with a frankly appraising concentration toward the window where Mario Maldonado was looking down at the city.

"Hi, honey," Chuck greeted Luz with an irritating attempt at flair. "Thanks for going with my baby here to see the new kid."

"No trouble," Luz murmured.

"Hey, Mario, I want you to meet two wonderful gals . . ."

"Luz and I have already met," Mario smiled.

"Is that so? But you haven't met my secretary, have you?" He grinned up at Rita possessively. "Rita Campos, meet Mercury's newest *artist*—Mario Maldonado."

While the usual pleasantries were exchanged, Luz was struck again by the absurd differences between the two men. It was obvious Mario had been working intensely on something because papers and notes were scattered all over a table on the far side of the room where he was standing. On the other hand, there were only a few glossy magazines spread out on Chuck's desk and practically nothing else except an empty coffee cup. Both were dressed casually and both had their shirts opened and their sleeves rolled up, but Mario looked cool and terribly attractive while Chuck managed only to look half-dressed and rather obscene. Rita was aware of the contrast, too. When Chuck tugged at her arm and attempted to pull her down to him, crooning, "Give us a kiss!", Rita suggested

63

instead, "Don't you want to know what we thought of Juanito Jimenez?"

"Sure, let's hear it," Chuck said, but he hadn't missed the put-off.

"He was sensational! And Luz thought so, too," she said artlessly. "He's built, funky, and dances up a storm!"

"We were aware of those facts," Mario cut in dryly, "but perhaps you noticed some pertinent details, Luz?" He stepped closer and smiled encouragement.

"I didn't know what to look for specifically, you understand?"

"Just give me your impressions."

"I would say he projected strongly, he had a well-modulated voice, and he seemed sharp and intelligent. However . . ."

"However, what? Tell me, Luz."

"It's just a hint of something I felt . . ."

"That's what I want to hear. Go on."

They might have been alone in the room, speaking, communing, relating only with each other, provoking in each other much more than merely an interchange of information.

"In spite of his bravado and machismo, I felt a touch of fear in him. Fear about what? I don't know, but maybe it's a quality the camera might pick up." It was so natural for her at this point to speak to him in their own language. *"¿Tú sabes de que estoy hablando, verdad, Mario?"*

"Sí, niña, yo sé . . . yo sé . . ." Mario Maldonado could well suspect what Juanito Jimenez might be fearing.

Chuck's sudden loud shout made Luz jump. "Great! Couldn't be better! He'll come through on the screen a little vulnerable, a little lost, and we'll exploit that—oh, baby!—how we'll exploit that! Women will want to mother him. They'll freak out!"

For the first time, Luz caught a glimpse of Mario's temper. "Exploit?" The word was soft, not hard, but

64

Chuck's shout a moment ago hadn't carried as much impact. "You haven't even met the kid yet, Chuck, and already you're planning to exploit him?"

"Hey, calm down! Just keep in mind that this kind of film making is a business and not high art."

Mario refused to reply to that, but he was seething. She could feel the fury vibrating through his body when he clutched her hand. "Let's take a walk, Luz." He led her quickly out of the office.

They walked rapidly along a maze of halls, turning right and then left, and on and on until Luz was completely disoriented.

"Mario . . . ?"

"Sh-h-h, I want to show you something." The anger had drained away as swiftly as it had surfaced.

"What is it? Can't you tell me where we're going?"

"If I told you, then I would spoil the surprise, wouldn't I?"

He continued to pull her along. He finally stopped in front of an impressive-looking door. It had an elegant brass plate on its grained surface and his name was deeply engraved in the rich metal.

"Your own office—oh, Mario, how wonderful!"

"Beats having to share an office with Chuck, anyway. Not that I'm ungrateful, but I'm afraid we're like oil and water." He flung the door open. "I want you to be my first visitor."

The room was large and beautifully wood-grained, and the floor was lushly carpeted in deep chocolate brown. Storage boxes filled with papers and books were the only articles in the room. "A very temperamental interior decorator will outfit the place with a fancy desk and some other stuff, but I don't care about that. All I want are files so I can put my papers away." He gravitated toward the floor-to-ceiling windows again as he had done in Chuck's office. The self-contained, insulating building seemed to be

65

suffocating him. "This is a long way from the *barrio*, isn't it?" His voice had a mocking lilt to it.

Luz remembered with a shudder that Juanito had asked almost the same question. She walked and stood next to him, shoulder to shoulder.

"You know, I've worked in a tin shed that froze my bones at night and baked my brains by day. I've shot thousands of feet of film in a damp warehouse, and I've even set up shop in a converted garage. But I always produced something of quality. I wonder what I will accomplish in this gaudy plastic palace."

"You'll go right on making great films, Mario. Only, they'll be major commercial films instead of documentaries, that's all."

"I hope you're right," he nodded wistfully. "But I forgot—you're my number-one fan, aren't you?"

"And when you're very, very famous, you'll probably also forget I discovered you first!"

"No I won't, Luz." He held her, and although he held her tightly, it was very different from the way he had held her last night. And when he kissed her, it was bittersweet and tender.

"What happened between you and your sister after I left? Nothing heavy, I hope?" he murmured finally.

She leaned her head on his shoulder, folding her arms lithely around his back, matching his mood.

"Nothing happened. In fact, all the fuss had nothing to do with you," she whispered, determined not to tell him the truth. Who would believe it, anyway?

"I called your office this afternoon, but your secretary said you had left for the day. At least, I *think* that's what she said. She was stammering and sneezing through the whole conversation."

"That was Betsy. She has allergy attacks when she gets emotionally worked up. Betsy is my assistant, not my secretary. I'm not important enough to have a secretary."

She smiled up at him and saw that wonderful twinkle spring back into his stunning eyes.

"Somebody in the front office seems to think *I'm* important enough to have a secretary. Interested?"

"Nope, sorry. I can't take shorthand and I'm much too independent." He would have absolutely no problem getting a secretary, she thought. The girls in the studio pool would probably trample each other in the rush to get the job. "But speaking of secretaries, I'd better get Rita home. She's in no condition to drive."

"Yeah, I noticed she looked a little blown away." He kissed her lips lightly, once, twice, then drew her to the door. "Can you handle her alone?" They began walking slowly back. "Why don't you let me take you both home? You live near each other, don't you?"

"Right down the same block. No, Mario, thanks, but I can manage her easily enough." She had been tempted for a second to say *yes,* but only because she wanted to remain close to him—like this, with his arm gripping her shoulder.

They found a sour scene when they got to Chuck's office. Rita's eyes were puffy, and Chuck wore the expression of a man who had just said something crude. He looked at Mario and Luz with almost a smile of relief. "Time everybody went home to their own little beds." But he was dead serious when he said, "Take her home, will you, Luz?" He started to roll down his sleeves. "Mario, the Jimenez kid will be in to see me at eleven. Want to sit in on it?"

"No, thanks." Mario didn't stoop to match Chuck's buddy-buddy tone. "You're the casting man. I'll let you know what I think afterward."

"Okay, have it your own way."

Luz reached for Rita's arm and looked at her closely. Rita looked miserable. The deep rings around her eyes, her trembling mouth, and her sagging body clearly reflected her misery. Luz's earlier anger instantly melted away and she felt a sweep of compassion. They had been true friends for a long time. Urgingly, she murmured, "We'd better go." Rita barely nodded her head.

"I'll walk you down to the car," Mario said, getting his jacket. "Thanks for the use of your office, Chuck." It was spoken sincerely, without any frills.

"Hey, my pleasure." Chuck's spirits seemed to be rebounding now that he was getting rid of Rita. They left him in his office, humming.

Mario guided Rita effortlessly down to the car and helped her sit down. He opened the door for Luz but leaned across it, blocking her way. "Have dinner with me tomorrow night?"

"I'd love that, but tomorrow's Friday, and I always help my sister at the bakery on Friday nights." She saw his slight frown, and rushed to plead, "It's her busiest night, and I would hate to leave her to face it alone, without warning. She works very hard, and I always help her as much as possible."

"I understand." He removed his arm, and she slipped in behind the wheel. "But leave this weekend free," he said, leaning over to look at her. She nodded quickly. He walked away, and she released the brake after glancing at Rita. She was fast asleep.

Luz had to shake her several times before Rita responded. "Are we home?"

"Yes." Luz slipped the ignition key into Rita's purse. Rita got out stiffly, mumbled something over her shoulder, and disappeared into her house. Luz stood motionless, wondering how much longer Rita could keep up this destructive kind of life. There was nothing else she could do for her friend tonight. Mario had been right. All she could do was be there when Rita would need her.

She turned her steps slowly toward her own house. The

night was beautiful and heavy with the scent of the ever-present jasmine, and again she thought of Mario and their stroll down picturesque Calle Olvera. Neighbors were sitting out in their yards enjoying the perfect evening. One after the other they greeted Luz, and she responded in turn, asking about their health and the health of their children and grandchildren. She knew them all, and they had watched Luz grow up into beautiful young womanhood.

She finally reached her house and walked in quietly, but stopped at Trina's bedroom door when she noticed a sliver of light showing beneath it. She opened the door a notch and whispered, "Still awake?"

"Yes, come on in, dear."

Her sister was sitting up in bed saying her rosary. Luz sat on the edge of the bed, and kissed Trina's cheek. "I've interrupted your prayers."

"It's not important—God is patient." She smiled at Luz. "Only youth is impatient." She was harboring some news, but was taking her time divulging it; Luz knew all her habits. "When people get older and gain God's wisdom, they either grow more patient or they become eccentric. Now take Jorge Garcia, for instance. I think it's possible he might turn eccentric." She laid her beads aside.

Luz simply waited. The last person she wanted to talk about was Jorge Garcia, but she showed remarkable patience for somebody so young.

"I don't know why, but he didn't stay too long after you left, Luz, which is very surprising. He also kept upsetting things, and he dropped one of my good coffee cups, smashing it to pieces." Trina did not acknowledge the smile that had sneaked up into Luz's face. "But he did ask me to assure you he held you, as ever, in his highest esteem. He swore he would never marry anyone else, and if you come to your senses, he'll be waiting for you in Mexico. I urge

69

you not to forget him, Luz. He might be getting a little eccentric, but he's still a good, honest man."

That lecherous old hypocrite wasn't eccentric, Luz almost blurted out, he was just plain nuts! But she didn't want to hurt Trina's feelings. Anyway, he was gone forever. Luz decided to keep her little secret about Jorge Garcia to herself for the time being.

"That young man who was kissing you so passionately last night—did he bring you home again?"

"No, I came home with Rita."

"Good, I'm glad she decided to spend one night this week under her mother's roof." Her eyes crackled with disgust. "Scandalous! Her behavior will kill her mother." She suddenly clutched Luz's hand so strongly that it hurt. "I don't want you to turn out like Rita."

"Trina, please, stop worrying." She broke the tight grip and pulled her hand back. "But you have to remember I'm not a little girl anymore."

"You're *my* sister, and you'll always be *my* responsibility! Our family is strange; it produces either saints or sinners. Your brother has led a good life and is a good priest, but I . . ." She reached for her beads and they gave her the comfort she needed at that moment. "What I mean is, you and I are very much alike, so I know what you're thinking and feeling." She reached out and kissed Luz with great warmth, and then said a very strange thing. Strange for Trina, anyway. "Last night, with that man, you weren't thinking at all, you were only feeling something so overpowering that—I had to stop you. I want you to be very, very happy, but I also want you to be respected and to be secure for the rest of your life. Do you understand?"

"Of course, I understand." What a peculiar mood her sister was in tonight! "It's late, Trina. Good night now, and sleep tight."

"Luz?"

"Yes?" She stopped at the door and turned to face Trina.

"That young man . . . what's his name?"

"Mario Maldonado."

"Does he work with you at the studio?"

"Yes, he'll be making his first feature film at Mercury. He's a writer and director. I'd like you to meet him." Luz hoped her sister would answer her silent plea.

"An artist?" Trina only reflected; the invitation had been deliberately withheld. "Does he live in the *barrio*?"

"No." Where *did* he live? "But he was born here." Why did that sound like she was making an excuse for him? "Now go to sleep. Tomorrow's a hard day for you. I'll be there to help you, as usual." Luz blew a kiss.

"Luz . . . ?"

"Let's not talk anymore tonight." Luz closed the door quickly.

I'll have a full day tomorrow, too, Luz realized, crossing the hall to her own room. She wanted to sleep for days and days. Of course, that luxury would be impossible, but after only another moment's hesitation, she picked up the phone and dialed her office number. Betsy's prerecorded voice answered, requesting the caller to leave a message, name, and phone number where Miss Rivas could reach the caller as soon as possible. "Betsy, this is Luz. I won't be in the office"—she glanced at her clock on the dresser—"today until noon. Call me at home if anything important comes up. Thanks."

Wicked, absolutely wicked. And irresponsible! But Luz kicked off her shoes then threw herself on her bed and laughed. She hadn't missed a day's work in months; taking three hours off was no sin, certainly. Settling deeper into the soft comforter covering the bed, she looked around her cozy room, sighting the familiar furniture, pictures, and mementos. The amber night light cast a glow throughout the room as delicate as the sun's very last setting light. On the window's ledge sat a straw doll and an old *jarrilla,* a chocolate cup with her name embossed on its side. She had brought both treasures along to her new home as a child. On the same ledge, she had set down the candle Mario had bought her in Olvera Street. Her eyes lingered on it for a while. What kind of scent did it have? Surely, it would have a very seductive name, something that would immediately conjure up a vision of a faraway place, a balmy night, and a dark, smoldering stranger. Very romantic and lyrical, very predictable and absurd! With her imagination playfully stirred, she sat up and lifted the candle off the ledge. Turning it over so that she could read the name of the perfume, she smiled to herself. Oh, yes, she had guessed right; it was called "Jardines de España." A small wedge of wax clung to the tip of her finger and she instantly recognized the released scent . . . it was plain old Southland jasmine again, that's all!

Luz flicked on the radio, tuning it low so its music would not disturb Trina, then she carried the silly little wax flower into the bathroom and deposited it on the vanity alongside assorted bottles of cologne and the pretty blue jar she had purchased impulsively one day while browsing through the artists' village down in Laguna. Rita had been with her, and Luz had bought the jar on Rita's insistence. Suddenly she remembered that Rita had later given her a gift of bath salts, which she had poured into the jar and had completely forgotten about, until now. With a whimsical sense of premonition, she lifted the jar's cover—and up rose the identical fragrance of jasmine. Well, if she was fated to be inundated with the scent, she might as well wallow in it, she decided, sprinkling some of the salts into the tub and turning on the tap. To top off the silliness, she lighted the wax flower and watched the flame quicken and swell as she slowly began to take off her clothes. The pallid light transformed her lovely skin from gold to alabaster, and a sigh of pure pleasure broke

72

through her lips as she succumbed to the warm inducement of the water.

Her body lay inert, but her mind raced with fleeting images; her first sight of Mario after being beguiled by his voice, the shine of his dampened hair that she had so yearned to touch—and when she had touched it later, so soft, so pleasurable—and his strange tenderness tonight. All Mario; her thoughts were only of him. Improbably, she realized with a sense of shock that she had met him only twenty-four hours ago. Bewildered, she realized at the same time that she was beginning to fall in love with him.

CHAPTER FOUR

Luz awoke feeling wonderful, but also feeling slightly guilty. The clock said it was ten-twenty yet it had been the sun's light that had awakened her and not the alarm; she had deliberately not set it.

Choosing what to wear this morning seemed to take longer than usual—for some odd reason. Finally, she decided on a frothy paisley dress that clung to her as she moved, light and cool. One last critical glance in the mirror and she left the house, knowing she looked quite sensational this particular morning.

Betsy shot out of the office just as Luz arrived at the studio. "I got your message this morning, but"—her voice dropped dramatically—"why didn't you warn me?"

"Warn you about *what*, Betsy?"

"About what's waiting for you in there. He's gorgeous!"

Juanito Jimenez, of course. Luz had completely forgotten he had insisted on coming around after the interview. "Look, Betsy, you know that weekly department meeting you're always begging me to attend? Why don't you take my place today?"

Betsy was more than resentful. Actually, she looked almost rebellious. "You don't want me in the way, right?"

Luz nodded. "I don't want you in the way, *right!* But it's not what you think. I have a feeling Juanito will be working here at the studio, and I promise next time he stops in, you can have him all to yourself. Now, do me this favor and cover for me at the meeting."

Betsy made an awful face. "I must be crazier than I thought, but . . ." She walked back into the office and came back immediately with a pile of scripts. "I'll hold you to your promise, Luz, because I think he's . . . !" Her mouth mimed a few words not normally spoken aloud in polite society when describing the finer points of the opposite sex.

Luz merely shook her head. She found Juanito stalking up and down the room, too nerved up to stand still or sit down. He spied Luz and broke into a very boyish grin. "I thought maybe you were trying to avoid me."

"I overslept." She smiled warmly, hoping he would calm down a bit. "How did the interview go?"

"Okay. I mean, I think it went okay. I couldn't get a good handle on it because that Harrison guy is a pretty slick fish." He suddenly didn't appear as self-contained as she remembered. "He told me the film's director will have to talk to me, then the two of them will get together and decide."

"Yes, he's Mario Maldonado."

74

"Latino?" He looked skeptical. *"¿Cosa rara, no? No se encuentran muchos de nosotros aquí."* He rolled his eyes indicating the heady height that was Mercury Studios.

"Es verdad, pero Mario es un hombre extraordinario."

"¿No me dígas . . . ?" But he was still not convinced.

"Coming from the *barrio* he had to fight a little harder, that's all. But I don't think he uses his background as an excuse when he fails at something." Luz leveled with him. "I don't think any of us should."

"Hey, Luz, you're not old enough to preach at me like my *mamacita.*" He easily fell back on his sex appeal. "In fact, I saw you at ringside last night and I said to myself, now there's a classy girl who doesn't remind me of my mother *at all!*" His manner wasn't all show . . . he could really turn it on. "Relax a little bit, stop being snooty, and I know we could have a good little thing going."

Luz sighed. Had she really expected anything else from him? "I know this will sound corny, but I'd like us to be friends."

"Yeah, well, that's exactly what I was saying," he murmured, letting his fingers slide teasingly down her arm. "I'd like us to be real friendly."

Subtlety was obviously not a method that would work well with Juanito, so she spoke plainly. "This may shock you, but I'm not interested, period." She had been right; he was shocked. "But I meant what I said about being your friend. In this business, believe me, you'll need all the friends you can get."

But he only answered brashly, "Get this, Luz. If I want friendship I'll hang out with my buddies—not women."

She shrugged. "It's your choice." Suddenly, she lost her temper with this arrogant boy. "Why don't you follow your own advice and just relax! And sit down!"

He sat, puzzled. Then, streetwise, he stumbled on the only reason he could half-accept for her cold shoulder.

"You got it strong for some other guy, eh, Luz?" His ego had been badly bruised.

He was so apparent that she had an impulse to laugh, but she knew that would be a grave mistake. Not knowing why, she admitted, "I—yes, there's somebody else."

"But?"

"I don't know what you mean by *but.*"

"I mean how does this guy feel about you?"

This had gone too far. But he had swiftly gone to the heart of her dilemma. Only two days ago she had met a man. Today she knew—as she had never known anything else in her life—that Mario Maldonado was very special to her. But, how did *he* feel about *her?*

Juanito was peering at her. "Feel like unloading? I've had a lot of experience in this sort of little thing, you know." He was crowing like a strutting rooster.

"No, I don't want to talk about it, or about me, understand? I really want you to tell me about yourself, and about your life. Do you mind?" An idea began to take shape in her mind, an idea that Betsy had reawakened yesterday.

Juanito shrugged and finally put aside his act for the moment. "I'm nothing special. Went to school in East L.A. like everybody else and dropped out too soon like everybody else. I could always dance, so I started looking around for a job as a disco jockey. I worked in a few flophouses, then landed the gig at Roxie's." Again he shrugged. "If I get this break . . ."

But she knew there was much more to his story. "You didn't build up that body by only fighting in the streets or dancing," she dared to speculate aloud. "Did you play basketball or something?"

"Yeah, I played ball and worked out in the gym at school. Mostly just for kicks, you know? But I got really hooked on gymnastics. The coach thought I had what it takes to go all the way, and I really began to get good."

76

His eyes became animated, and he was back in that school gym for the moment. "Coach worked with me night and day. I made the school team right away, and then I made all-city. You won't believe this," he snorted, "but a number of scouts from the big colleges had a look at me."

"Why shouldn't I believe you?" She had been listening to him intensely, so it was just by chance that her eyes flickered past him and she saw Mario leaning against the door frame. He silently signaled for her not to acknowledge he was there—and to keep Juanito talking. Her eyes darted back to the boy, but he had noticed nothing. He was still wrapped in his one moment of glory. "What happened then, Juanito?" she asked carefully, willing herself not to look at Mario. It wasn't easy. How long had he been standing there?

"Nothing happened! I wasn't cut out for all that college jazz." Juanito laughed jarringly and assumed his cocksure stance again. "Too much training, too much clean living, well, that's not my style, you know what I mean? I couldn't stick to training while all my buddies were having a great time with the girls, could I? So I broke training a few times, and my coach counted me out." He squared his shoulders. "No big thing, right? Anyway, I don't mind what I'm doing. It brings in the bucks."

"Sometimes." Mario walked in. "Hello. I'm Mario Maldonado." The two men shook hands, and Mario sat down comfortably nearby. They sized each other up for a second, and it was Juanito's eyes that fell first. Only then did Mario smile over to Luz, but for her the smile said everything.

With a few short questions, Mario skillfully gauged Juanito's show-business experiences, digging deep and getting all the information he needed. But Luz also knew he was looking for something only intuition could tell him. At last Mario said, "I'll talk with Chuck Harrison. If we both agree you're right for the part, then the studio will contact you. Offhand, I would say your chances look pretty good.".

Juanito seemed slightly shaken by Mario's last remark, but tried to cover quickly. "Sounds okay." He finally gave in to a grin. "Thanks, Mr. Maldonado!"

"First lesson," Mario said, shaking his head, "is to learn to call everybody by their first name. I'm Mario, you're Juanito, and she's Luz." The three of them suddenly laughed at the trio of Spanish names, and the tension washed away from Juanito's face. But his antennae had picked up the indirect but very strong waves between Mario and Luz. He stood up quickly. "Uh-h, I'd better be going. Thanks again . . . Mario!" He turned his face toward Luz so that Mario could not see, and he winked, implying his expertise on such matters. " 'Bye, Luz. Good luck with *everything.* "

She waved good-bye and watched him leave. "I must confess I hope you give him the part, Mario."

"He's rough and raw, and I'll have to work hard to smooth the edges, but I think he's the one."

"I'm so glad. How did you know he was here?"

"Rita told me."

"Oh?" She could easily picture Rita purring like a damned cat, hoping Mario would catch her and Juanito on the couch.

"Yeah, I stopped in to see Chuck because he left me a message that he wanted to talk to me about Juanito as soon as possible, but I just missed him. Rita told me he had an urgent appointment at the Marina." His dry smile told her more or less what he thought of Chuck's urgent business at the famous yachting spot. "I suppose he's suddenly afraid he'll lose his job, so he's become anxious to finish casting this project. Some people never learn," he snapped, letting his contempt show, "until they're burnt. He expects to do in one day what he should have been doing for weeks. Anyway, he'll just have to wait until

Monday to catch me." He unexpectedly looked at her mouth in a way that made her feel dizzy. "I'm glad I saw Juanito . . . but that's not why I came here."

"Don't tell me," she whispered tauntingly. "You fell in love with Betsy's voice and you couldn't keep away."

"How did you guess?" He leaned toward her and kissed her quickly but thoroughly. "Where is she? Gone home for the day, I hope?" He bent his head preparing to take her mouth at a more leisurely pace, but she eluded the temptation. "Covering for me at a meeting, but she should come bounding in here any moment."

He reluctantly released her. "I have a meeting, too, so I'd better be going. I only stopped in to remind you about our date for tomorrow."

"I haven't forgotten."

"Sure you won't change your mind and have dinner with me tonight?"

"Mario, I can't. I have to help my sister, believe me."

"Okay, see you tomorrow." He turned to leave, but stopped when he noticed a pile of scripts on her desk. "Don't you get tired reading other people's work all day long?"

"I certainly do! I sometimes want to tear the whole stack to shreds." Suddenly, she knew she had to ask. If he hadn't mentioned the scripts she would have never thought about it. "Mario, can I ask your opinion about something? It'll only take a second."

"Of course." He saw that she was nervous. "Is it important?"

"Very important, but I know you have to leave . . ."

Without another word, he picked up her phone and asked to be connected to the vice-president of the studio. Simply and directly, not giving the VP a chance to ask questions, he stated he would be held up for a few minutes longer, and hung up the phone. "Now what is it, Luz?"

Thrilled by his nerve, she forced up her own resolve. "I've wanted to write my own script for years, but I never could find the right format or direction. Or subject, either." She faltered.

He urged her on softly. "Yes?"

"I suppose your documentaries first gave me the idea, but I didn't think I could ever write anything even half as good." She smiled nervously and shook her head, amazed at what she was confessing. "I know now I want to write like you, and I want to write about Juanito and his life in the *barrio.*" She timidly glanced into his eyes. "Do you think I should try?"

"Not only do I think you should try, but I'll help you as much as I can."

"I hadn't hoped for so much—thank you!"

"Don't thank me so soon. I expect you to work hard. I'll send over some of my notes and scripts. Look them over. When you come to my place tomorrow, I want you to bring along anything you've written so that I can get an idea of your work. Oh, and don't forget your bathing suit."

"Your place—and bring my bathing suit?"

"Sure. My place at eleven-thirty sharp. We'll have brunch, and then you'll have your first writing lesson while we stretch out on the sand." He laughed at her expression. "Didn't you know I live at the beach? Here's my address," he said, writing hurriedly and dropping the paper on her desk. "Eleven-thirty, and Luz . . . don't plan on leaving early, understand?"

She knew exactly what he meant. An insidious ache spread down throughout her body. "Mario . . ."

He moved to kiss her, *really* kiss her this time, but Betsy made one of her most ill-timed, aggravating entrances. Puffing under a pile of scripts and notes, she wailed, "I think I'm going to die! I swear, Luz, I'm pooped, and I just want to . . . !" She stopped, took one look at Mario and

Luz, and all the papers went crashing down on the desk. Her earlier brief encounter with Juanito had seriously jolted her jittery libido, but now her nerves completely self-destructed.

Luz pushed herself out of Mario's arms and managed an introduction, or something close to an introduction. Betsy couldn't even get out a squeak, so Mario came to the rescue. "Ah, yes, Betsy! You're the gal with the sexy voice on the phone, aren't you!" He then gave Luz one last look and walked out.

"Pull yourself together, Betsy. You're practically drooling." Luz sat down with determination and began earnestly looking through some memos. She didn't know what she was reading. Mario's closeness was still too real.

Betsy gulped. "Hey, *hey*, now! *You* weren't exactly acting cool as a cucumber when I walked in here, either, you know!" She sat down at her typewriter and whispered in awe, "I thought Juanito was too much, but compared to your Mario, he's . . ." She snapped her fingers contemptuously.

Luz continued to ignore her, and soon Betsy calmed down. But every once in a while, Betsy peeked over as if trying to figure out the mystery of Luz's devastating allure.

The phone rang and Luz picked it up before Betsy could beat her to it. It was Trina. "Luz, you don't have to help me at the bakery tonight. Aren't you happy, dear? Mrs. Campos said she would be glad to take your place. Actually, I think she was looking for an excuse to get out of the house for a few hours—and get some rest. Luz, did you hear me?"

"Yes, I heard what you said." She fought down a terrible sense of near-panic and disappointment. She could have had dinner with Mario after all. Perhaps it wasn't too late. *No,* she realized it was too late by now. Besides, calling him now would only make her appear childish and anxious. "It was good of Mrs. Campos to want to help. I have lots of work. Now I can catch up."

"Must you work, Luz? Why don't you go home, rest, and take it easy?"

"I'm not tired. Really, Trina."

"All right, dear. I'll see you later at home."

"Fine. Good-bye."

She hung up feeling totally drained. She needed desperately to be alone. "Betsy, you've done enough for today. Why don't you go home?"

"Sounds great to me. Now I can beat the traffic." She scurried around before Luz had a chance to change her mind and gathered together all her stuff. " 'Bye," she shouted from the doorway. "Have a fabulous weekend, and I'll see you Monday morning."

It took a few minutes for everything to stop vibrating after Betsy left. Where would the girl spend her weekend, Luz wondered? Would she be alone, or would she be tracking down some guy in a singles bar? Thoughts of Rita sprang to mind, and she pushed them away. *Stop,* she told herself, and dug right back into her work.

The knocking on the door became insistent. Luz called out for whoever it was to come on in, and Mickey poked her head around the doorjamb. "I was about to give up," Mickey said in her whiskey-sour voice. "Are you getting deaf in your old age?"

Mickey's real name was Melissande, but no one in his or her right mind would dare call her anything but "Mickey." She was the studio's best secretary, fifty years old, skinny as a rail, and was now working on her fourth divorce. Mickey had seen it *all.* She wasn't just hard—she was granite.

"I was really concentrating, I guess," Luz smiled, brightening at the reference to age. "What brings you around here?"

"My new boss asked me to bring this over to you," she replied with a shake of her dyed iodine-red hair, but there was a kindness in her look when she spoke to Luz.

"Let's see what you have." Luz took the portfolio, wondering which executive had cornered Mickey's skills this time; she could pick and choose. Opening the case, Luz drew out a batch of clipped sheets—and gaped in amazement when she saw Mario's name on every one of the pages.

"Your *boss? You're* Mario's new secretary?"

"Sure," Mickey rasped, "he picked me for my sex appeal." She broke out in a horselaugh. "I tell you, there are a dozen young things around this studio who would just as soon see me drop dead!"

Her wry humor was infectious, and Luz found herself bursting out laughing. "Thanks, Mickey."

"My pleasure, Luz. I guess we'll be seeing a lot of each other, right?" She didn't wait for Luz's reply, and slammed the door shut quickly.

Luz was still shaking her head over Mario's choice minutes after Mickey had left. Then she spread out his outlines, and was gripped by the material from the very first page. Hour after hour sped by.

The drive to the beach was sheer pleasure. The closer she got to the ocean, the more exhilarated she became, and the bright sun also played its part in her joyfulness. Taking the Lincoln Boulevard exit off the freeway, she turned left, heading toward Venice, and instantly got caught in the old Coast Highway's usual bumper-to-bumper traffic. She wasn't in the least bit frazzled; nothing could spoil her day. Eventually she worked her way down through the traffic and headed in the direction of the water, but then she became almost totally lost in the intricate streets that bordered the old canals. She stopped the car and re-checked the address Mario had scribbled down. Well, she was on the correct street, anyway, but the house number made no sense at all. The beach itself was very narrow at this point, and the ocean came very close to the street. The only building she could see corresponding to the address Mario had given her was a quaint old-style firehouse made entirely of salt-bleached bricks. She locked the car and had just about decided to hunt for a telephone when she saw Mario wave to her from the top floor of the firehouse.

"I'll be right down," he shouted, and disappeared. Seconds later he reappeared out in front of the building and ran to her.

"Don't tell me you actually live in a firehouse!" she laughed, while he was still about ten feet away.

"Sure I do," he beamed, "and it's the choicest spot on the beach." He closed the gap between them swiftly and hugged her to his body. "Mm-m-m, you feel good," he muttered, hugging her tighter. "And you look good, too!"

She had agonized for an hour this morning over the simple problem of which shorts and top to wear. Because she had suddenly pictured Rita doing the same thing the night of Chuck's party, she had cursed herself for being a ninny and had put on her original choice. What had first driven her to reject that particular ensemble was that the shorts were way too short, and the tube top was a mere bagatelle that made little attempt to cover her small but beautifully rounded breasts. Now, basking in Mario's admiring gaze, she was glad she had found the nerve to stick to her original choice.

"I thought we'd get something to eat first," he said, removing her large beach bag from the car, "and then I can show you my house. Sound okay?"

"Sounds great. I'm starving."

They neared the firehouse and Mario said, "I'll just drop this off inside." He entered the place and left her bag in the front hallway, then came back quickly, leaving the front door opened and unlocked.

84

"You forgot to close the door," Luz reminded him.

"Nobody locks anything around here. Don't worry, I promise your things will be safe." He took her by the hand, and they walked on to the paved pathway bordering the beach itself. An iron rack stacked with rather dilapidated bicycles was located nearby, and Mario pointed to it. "Choose one."

"Just any bicycle?" Luz asked surprised. "Don't they belong to anybody?"

He was already astride one of the bikes. "They belong to everybody who lives out here. We share, then leave them along the beach when we're finished using them," he explained. "Come on."

They pedaled side by side at a good pace, but both carefully avoided wandering out of the marked bike-path because of the carefree roller skaters who glided along beside them. Luz looked over at the sea, green and luminous now that the sun was directly overhead, and then she scanned the miles and miles of tawny beaches. A beautiful day, and a beautiful way to share it, with Mario. He was smiling at something she had said, and she was struck again by his charisma. The white tight ducks and T-shirt only added to his attraction.

"The restaurant's right ahead." he signaled as they passed a mall filled with shops and people. Luz pulled in to follow him to an area where they parked the bikes and walked a short distance along the beachfront to the restaurant.

She found herself seated at a small table facing Mario—surrounded by stacks and stacks of books!

"Why are you smiling at me that way, Luz?"

"Because you amaze me!" She shook her head and enjoyed the way he had folded his fingers around her arm. "First you took me to a wonderful *puesto* in Olvera Street that just happened to have my name, then I found you living in a firehouse, and now you bring me to have brunch in a library!"

"Like it?"

"It's beautiful."

The unique eatery was a combination restaurant and bookstore, and it was also a browser's paradise. The clients sat sipping coffee or wine, or indulged in delightful meals while reading from the displayed assortment of books, magazines, and newspapers.

The waiter who came to take their order was dressed as casually as most of the patrons. Luz glanced at the two-foot-long menu. Mario watched her, amused. "You order for me," she pleaded, perplexed.

"Do you trust me?"

"I have no choice. I don't know what any of these things mean!"

After a second's thought, he ordered something akin to two Paradise Losts and two Strawberry Waltzes.

"I suppose you won't tell me what you *really* ordered?"

"Nope. It'll spoil the surprise."

Their meal arrived, and it turned out to be both a visual and taste treat: fluffy omelettes stuffed with crab and avocados, and delightfully refreshing drinks of orange juice, champagne, and crushed strawberries.

Luz was impressed by the easy, untroubled atmosphere of the life-style along the beach. "Everyone is so unconcerned and informal around here."

"Rule number one is that there shall be *no* rules, period. As long as everybody's property and privacy is respected, then we have no need for rules and regulations," Mario explained with a grin. "But there are other things that do need guides and rules. Did you have a chance to look through the outlines I sent to your office?" The grin turned into a broad smile. "And what did you think of my new secretary?"

"I was dumbfounded. How did you settle on Mickey?"

"I didn't choose Mickey. Mickey chose me. She marched right up to me and demanded to know if I wanted to fool around with just another pretty face, or did I want the best damned secretary at the studio, meaning herself! How could I resist her?"

"You certainly picked right. Mickey is a gem." She sipped some champagne and stated another fact. "I read through all your outlines, and they are absolutely brilliant."

"You had time to read all of them last night?"

She couldn't bring herself to admit that she hadn't worked at the bakery after all, so she used the excuse, "I read fast and I know how to spot important details. Don't forget, I'm a script analyst."

Again, he took her praise completely in stride, but seemed to be concerned with another matter altogether. "Well, let's hope you're not stuck as a script reader forever. Did you bring along anything you've written?"

"Yes, I did." Now it was her turn to be mysterious. "I brought something else for you, too."

"For me? What, Luz?"

"If I told you, it would spoil the surprise, wouldn't it?"

He feigned submission for a second. But the next moment brought a mocking glint to his eyes. "I'm cursed by impudent women—first Mickey, now you. I guess I'll have to teach you both who's boss. Each in a different way, of course."

"Why, I thought you didn't believe in rules and regulations," she innocently countered.

"For you, I have something more direct in mind . . ." His voice trailed off. "But not now. Now let's go back and soak up some sun. I'll read your work while we're on the beach."

Their original bikes had been claimed by other folks, just as he had foretold, and they helped themselves to another pair. The beach had become crowded, so they rode back with only an occasional word or smile, keeping their sights mostly on the others using the path.

The firehouse came into view, and they left the bikes at the rack, walking homeward arm in arm. "Now I'll give you the grand tour," he promised as they entered the front hallway, hoisting Luz's beach bag off the floor.

"The ground floor has been left pretty much as it was when this was the area's only fire station. Right now, it's rented to an artist who paints very large pictures."

Luz could see why this particular artist needed the space afforded by the high ceilings; the paintings were huge, one of them taking up an entire wall.

"He's off in Yucatan, sketching the Mayan ruins, or something, and won't be back for months, so I have the whole place to myself." He shut the front door, but Luz didn't comment this time when he again left it unlocked. "My apartment's upstairs."

He led her up a winding oak stairway, gleaming with wax and polish. The banister was fashioned entirely from brass. So solidly built was the whole structure that the wooden steps supported their climb without one creak or sound. "Well, Luz, how do you like it?"

She was standing under a large fan-shaped skylight that enticed the sun's brilliance to shine through instead of restricting it, and the place was flooded with light. Floors, ceilings, and window shutters all glowed with the warmth of hardwood, and the white walls showed up even more pristine against the depth of the wood. The whole apartment seemed to consist of one unbelievably large room, simply but stunningly furnished.

As she wandered farther into this astounding room, she noticed quite a number of small art objects, all exquisite, all in harmony with the surrounding space. A grand antique belly stove commanded one side of the room, and it looked quite capable of heating the entire firehouse, and beyond. The opposite wall was devoted completely to a small, enchanting del Poso lithograph.

She turned and faced Mario. "I think this is the most beautiful room I've ever seen."

He seemed to have been holding his breath slightly, waiting for her opinion. "I'm glad you like it so much."

"Don't you have a kitchen or bedroom?" she asked, gazing around again and noticing no evidence of either.

"Of course, I do." He walked to the far side and swung open a series of folding wooden doors beyond which was a bedroom consisting mainly of a large square-shaped bed in the dead center of the room. "And here's the kitchen." Again, a section of folding doors were pulled aside, and a complete kitchen came into view. "It has all the original fixtures, right down to the brass sink," he said as Luz came over to peek.

"It's all marvelous, Mario." Admiring the kitchen, she suddenly remembered something. "Ah, now I can give you your surprise." He was still holding onto her beach bag. "Here, let me have that," she said, and after he set it on the counter she delved into it, bringing out first a thick envelope. "These are my notes."

"Good." He took them from her. "But," he smiled, "where's my surprise?"

"Here." She brought forth a good-sized confectionery box tied very neatly with pink twine. "Well, aren't you going to open it?"

Putting the envelope aside, he very seriously accepted the gift, and then snapped the string apart with a twist of his long, strong fingers. Inside, delectably round and sugared and smelling heavenly, were an assortment of his favorite *panes de huevo.* "So you didn't forget," he marveled, unable to resist the temptation of breaking off a few crumbs to taste the cake. "It's wonderful," he murmured, laying the box aside, "and you're pretty wonderful, too, darling, thanks."

89

She savored the tender word. "You promised me a gallon of coffee, remember?"

"Sure do, and as soon as we get back from the beach, you'll have it." He picked up a pair of cutoffs from a nearby chair. "I'll change here and wait for you by the breakwater. If you insist on being modest you can use the bedroom." He was grinning rather sardonically as he began to slide the white ducks from his waist.

She retrieved her beach bag, headed for the bedroom, and tossed over her shoulder, "See you in a few minutes." She didn't look back. Once in the other room, she took her time undressing. Tying the three tiny strings that held her bikini together at the same slow pace, she then swept her long hair over high on her head and secured the heavy mass with a ribbon. Was he still standing just beyond the partly closed folding doors, she wondered? Then she realized that because of the muffled acoustics of the place, he had probably left without making a sound. She scooped up a few articles she'd be needing on the beach, folded the bedroom doors all the way back, and light-heartedly left the apartment.

Finding Mario was no problem at all. The huge boulders that formed the breakwater curved to almost enclose a section along the edge of the water, and the area was uncrowded. The only other people around were a boy training his dog to bring back sticks out of the water and a group of teenagers playing volleyball. Mario had spread a beach blanket out and was sitting with his back propped against one of the boulders. He seemed deeply engrossed in reading.

The scene was so peaceful and lovely that Luz halted for a second to enjoy it fully. The crash of the surf muted the happy barks of the dog and the shouts of delighted laughter arising from the athletic youngsters, and she gazed for a moment longer at Mario. He had obviously taken a quick dip in the ocean for his hair was still wet, and his copper skin still shone with moisture. Just as she was watching, he looked up at her. "Are you going in?" he asked, nodding toward the surf.

"No, I'm sure the water is too cold." She knelt down next to him. "Don't you mind the coldness?"

"No, I actually enjoy it."

She didn't need his acutely frank gaze to let her know she looked quite beautiful in her scant bikini, but she silently reveled in his response, anyway. "Don't let me disturb you," she insisted, stretching herself out full length on the blanket. "Please go on with your reading."

"You've got to be putting me on." His voice had become not only low but also husky. Although she had closed her eyes, she could sense he had stirred closer. "How the hell do you expect me to concentrate on a bunch of words with you lying next to me—looking like this . . ."

"If you don't concentrate on my scribblings, then you'll be condemning me to a lifetime of reading dull scripts, and I'll turn into a shortsighted, cranky old bookworm. You don't want that to happen, do you?" She glanced up at him.

"God forbid!" But he couldn't stop himself from gazing down the full length of her beautiful body again. Her sun-warmed skin drew him down to her like a magnet. His lips found the velvet-soft hollow at the base of her throat, and without rushing, without roughness, he worked her skin seductively beneath his mouth's pressure. Lifting her arms ever so slowly, almost in rhythm with his breathing, she threaded her fingers through his dark hair and sustained him there for a moment longer. Perhaps, a moment too long. She pulled his head back. "Mario, later . . . I promise."

He believed her. Later, after one more light kiss, he leaned away. "All right," he murmured gathering the papers, "but sit up, okay?"

She sat up straight. It helped, but not much. "What do you think of my writing?"

"It's good."

They spent the next few hours discussing the subject of writing outlines and scripts. Mostly, Luz listened and Mario talked. The sun had begun to slant, and the boy, the dog, and the teenagers had left. The sea breeze turned cooler.

"That's enough lecturing," he said finally. "The only way to learn to write is to write. We'll go on working next week." He stood up and helped her to her feet. "Now how about that coffee I promised you?"

The apartment was bathed in the sunset's light. In a little while the sun would disappear altogether, and then that first evening tint would cover everything in melancholy. Luz turned away from the window and accepted the steaming cup from Mario.

"You haven't even tasted my coffee yet," he jested, "so why do you look so unhappy?"

"I'm not unhappy. This has been the loveliest day, Mario."

"Has been?" He extended his arm to the window frame, leaning slightly, and encircling her within the curve of his body. She smiled, but nevertheless, the silent shudder couldn't be hidden. "Darling, what's the matter?"

She laughed at her own weaknesses. "Nothing, please believe me. It's just that I've never liked the hours between sunset and darkness. I know it sounds absurd," she attempted to explain, "but . . ."

"Nothing you say sounds absurd to me, Luz. I like everything about you." He brushed her hair away from her face. "Come away from the window."

He led her to the middle of the room and they sat down together amid a mound of floor cushions. "This coffee is good," she said, taking a sip, her eyes twinkling. "It was worth waiting for."

"Enjoy it then. It's the only cup I'm giving you, at least for a while, anyway. *Later.* That's what you whispered to me out there on the sands, remember?"

She hadn't forgotten, but she tensed, conscious of her own heartbeats. He took the brimming cup out of her fingers and then held her head tightly between his palms. "Remember?" he demanded to know, forcing her face to be within inches of his own. "Stop feeling uneasy," he whispered, lifting her face so that her eyes met his. "It can all end right now, if that's what you want."

"That's not what I want."

The uneven pulse of his words came to her then and stabbed at her with a pleasure so real, so urgent that she swayed out of his arms. Was it alarm or excitement that drove her to go beyond to the other part of the room to finally stand beside his bed? Whether from doubt or anticipation, she fumbled with the flimsy ties holding together the trivial stuff around her breasts and hips, and watched him come to her.

"No. Let me do that . . ."

Her fingers were snatched away from the cloth when he pinned both her arms in one hand and slid the other hand down along her spine in tormenting slowness from her neck to her waist. The cadence of the caress paralyzed her, and she crumbled to fall beneath him as they sank back on the bed.

"Did you really think I would let you go now?"

"I don't know what I was thinking . . ."

"Don't think . . . not now . . ." He gave her his open mouth, and her freed hands flew to catch his bare shoulders and back. With a deliberation that was maddening, he wound the futile little strings around his fingers until they snapped, and the thin cloth that separated her flesh from his dropped away. Enmeshed, her head pushed back

93

under his mouth, he explored and memorized every turn, curve, and dip of her body until her need became an ache that burned both of them. She arched herself upward, moaning under the pressure of his hunger. The tiny furrows she was etching along his back with the pointed tips of her fingernails stung just enough that he gasped, releasing her bruised mouth, but further arousing the desire he could no longer control. "Tell me . . . say it . . ." he breathed, demanding that each and every one of their senses be fulfilled and gratified. Far from being satiated, she told him, but her eyes remained closed.

"Don't close your eyes. Open them . . . keep looking at me . . ."

She couldn't see his face for he had become a dark silhouette against the last of the light, but his persuasive lips induced spirals of such pure stimulation wherever they touched her that at last she cried out his name and wrenched her head forward.

The shadows moved. Through her daze, she saw them move. It wasn't possible, yet they *had* moved. "Mario . . . !"

She had pushed him away suddenly, almost with cruelty. His reaction was slow and drugged. At first he misunderstood her panic, but then her almost lifeless rigidity convinced him that something was very wrong. He spun around.

Rita stood in the center of the lovely room, and Chuck Harrison was standing a few feet behind her, wearing a very dirty grin.

Mario moved quickly, then. He reached for the folding doors and slammed them shut behind him, cutting off the bedroom from the rest of the apartment. "What the hell are you two doing here?"

"Hey, we just thought we'd drop by. I mean, *Rita thought* it would be a good idea . . ." Chuck very stupidly continued to grin.

"Do you always just barge in like this?" Mario's voice was cold and dangerous.

It was Rita who answered. "We knocked. The front door was wide open." There was a strange, spiteful glint in her eye as she continued to glance toward the bedroom.

"Yeah, that's right," Chuck agreed in a rush, "and I even called out to you! But—I can see why you didn't hear me!" He obscenely let out a low whistle, but gulped it back swiftly when Mario appeared to step closer.

Instead, Mario turned and switched on a lamp on a nearby table. Then he faced Chuck again. "Just a friendly visit, huh?"

"Well, ah-h-h, I missed you at the studio yesterday, and Rita and I were out sailing at the Marina in my new sailboat, so I figured you and I could have a quick chat about the Jimenez kid. And this way I could start the ball rolling early on Monday . . . Damn it, Mario, you don't know how important this picture is for me!

"I don't know, and I don't care. Now shut up, and get out."

Something mean jumped into Chuck's face, but then he grinned again. "Sure! Hey, I'm sorry, okay, pal?"

Mario's face remained a cold mask and he said nothing. The silence went on for a beat. Rita hadn't moved one muscle all through the exchange between the two men.

"Come on, honey, let's go." Chuck grabbed Rita roughly by the arm and pulled her to the head of the stairs. He couldn't resist one last bit of bravado, however. "See you early Monday, right? That is, if you survive the weekend." Rita's shrill laugh remained in the room even after the front door banged closed with a crash.

Mario's hands were taut with tension when he pushed against the doors. He saw Luz had dressed, and she was methodically but unconsciously putting her things into the beach bag. He very carefully touched her hand. It was cold. Her eyes were frozen with shock.

"Darling, please," he whispered.

She flinched and turned away. "Don't say anything." She pulled her hand away, too. "I just want to get home."

He immediately caught the dangerous tone in her voice that told him how close she was to hysteria. "I don't want you to go home. Not just yet, anyway." He knew better than to try to touch her again. But he yearned to hold her and comfort her. "Wait," he pleaded, "and then I'll drive you home. We can leave your car here until tomorrow."

"No, I can drive myself home, thank you."

When she walked out of the bedroom, he almost gave in to the impulse to stop her, to stop her even if it meant physically holding her back, but he didn't dare risk it. Instead he murmured as softly as he could, "I care a great deal about you, and I don't give a damn what anybody else thinks. Do you believe me?"

She slowed her steps, but gave no other sign that he had reached her numbed heart and brain.

"I want . . ." Improbably, his voice seemed to dry in his throat, and he said the only thing that came into his mind. "I want to start helping you with your script as soon as possible. Will you let me do that?"

This time she halted, waited, and then nodded ever so little. "Oh, Mario, I'm so sorry," she sobbed all of a sudden, and then she was gone.

CHAPTER FIVE

"So I said to him, 'You bet!,' and we went to his place! Luz, are you listening to me?" Betsy asked.

"Yes, of course. You met this great guy Saturday night at the One-on-One Bar."

"Yeah, so we went to his place . . ."

Luz shut her eyes. If she could only keep herself from screaming at Betsy! Poor Betsy. It wasn't her fault that Luz couldn't stop from shaking inside. She forced herself to pay attention to Betsy's babbling, but her mind's eye gave her no peace. The terrible picture came back to haunt her again and again. She saw Rita glaring at her for that split second before Mario had mercifully shut the bed-room doors, and the message had been loud and clear. Don't you *ever again dare* to preach to me, my dear *innocent* friend!

". . . and isn't that the funniest thing you've ever heard!" Betsy howled.

"Absolutely hysterical," Luz answered mechanically, not having heard one word. And Mario? What had he been feeling after she left? And yesterday. Had he thought about her yesterday? She had spent the whole day doing nothing else.

"Luz, you look like you've seen a ghost. I swear, you've been acting weird all morning!"

"I'm going for a walk." She stood up abruptly. "Take down any messages, will you?"

"Sure, but . . ."

"I'm all right. Don't worry."

She headed directly for the large park in the center of the complex. She often went there when she wanted to be alone, or when she had a specific problem to work out. The trees offered shade and coolness, and the many sidepaths usually were bordered in multicolored blooms; all in all, a quiet retreat.

Luz found an isolated bench by a fountain and watched while a pair of birds gave themselves a very thorough bath. When they flew away, she suddenly felt empty and lonely. She had felt the same way all day yesterday, curled up in her favorite chair by her bedroom window. Being that it was Sunday, Trina had spent the day at church, first attending Mass, then helping serve food at the weekly bazaar. The phone had rung a number of times, but Luz had not left her chair to answer. She wondered if Mario had tried to call her.

"I tried to reach you all day yesterday."

She looked up into his dark eyes and felt her heart leap, stop, and then leap again. "How did you find me here?"

"Betsy told me." He smiled that slow, warm smile. "She seems to know your moods and habits. She was sneezing badly." The smile faded away, and his face showed a concern that was surprising. "I've been worried about you. I must have cursed myself a dozen times for letting you go home alone—for letting you go home at all."

"I—I wasn't home because—I was helping my sister at the church bazaar." Another lie; a terrible lie. Because she was falling in love with him, did that mean she would now compound lie upon lie? Would she become trapped in her own lies like Rita? And now she was beginning to do another horrible thing. She had begun to involve Trina in her lies. Trina. Trina and Rita. If Rita ever needed a weapon that could really wound, she could tell Trina about . . .

"Listen to me, Luz. It was very dark . . ."

"They saw. It wasn't that dark."

He began to shake his head in protest, but she quickly swept away that myth. "Mario, don't you remember? Rita was in the car when you asked me to spend the weekend with you. Because she knew . . . we'd be together, she forced Chuck to go to your apartment. Oh, yes, Mario, she *knew.*"

Frustrated, he said hotly, "But what the hell difference does it make!" A second later, he caught his breath and immediately looked contrite. "I'm sorry, that was crude and insensitive."

"No, you couldn't be crude or insensitive if you tried."

If she could only tell him she was not ashamed of her love for him. Yes, she loved him. She was honest enough with herself to realize that the most bitter regret of all was that he had been forced to stop making love to her. She had wanted more; she *still* wanted so much more! While he—he might be angry and frustrated, even compassionate and concerned, but he had said nothing about love. They had met casually only a few days ago, he had offered to help her with her writing, and he had been sexually attracted to her. For him, that's all there was to it. She felt convinced if she didn't keep her true feelings and fears to herself, she was in peril of losing even his friendship. Mario was the kind of independent man who would soon lose interest in any woman who attempted to possess him. "Maybe you're right," she smiled with as much conviction as she could muster. "Let's forget about it."

He walked slowly up the path a little way, his hands in his pockets, his eyes following the contour of the narrow walkway. Luz's sudden indifference didn't fool him in the least. He knew enough about her background—his background, too—to guess at what was really bothering her. The Hispanic code of morality was strong and unbreakable, and she had been brought up very rigidly within the

99

laws of that code. When she had so spontaneously and so excitingly responded to his own quickly triggered passion she had been at war with her innermost self. Why on earth should that bother him, he suddenly wondered? He retraced his steps feeling uneasy and puzzled. Luz was gazing at a small whirlwind of leaves in the fountain, and he scanned her profile. She was beautiful, but she was also very proud. He knew he must never do anything that might shatter that pride, so he changed the subject to fit her assumed mood. "We've decided to contract Juanito. I thought you'd like to know."

"I'm very happy for him," she replied with all honesty, "and for you, too."

"Are you still serious about writing that documentary?"

"Oh, yes. I have to learn more about Juanito, however."

"We start filming this week. I want you to talk to him on the set whenever you can. This way, it'll make things a little easier for Juanito." For Juanito, or for himself?

"Thanks so much, but won't I be in the way? I thought you always insisted on a closed set."

"Rules are made to be broken, remember?"

She murmured almost too quickly, "Well, I think I've left Betsy doing all the work long enough. I'd better get back to the office."

She turned away, but he stopped her. "I'll drop into your office whenever I get the chance to help with the script, okay?" She nodded, and he watched her walk away. Sometime later he realized he had better get to work, too.

Luz parked her car in the space reserved for visitors and then approached the gate's guard for directions to the sound stage. "You go right in, Miss Rivas," he nodded, "and you'll find Mr. Maldonado shooting on Stage ten."

Following the guard's very detailed instructions, she

wove her way along what appeared to be a self-contained city. She seldom wandered on the lot among the stages for her work was largely centered in the front offices. The "streets" here were paved and numbered, and signposts pointed to everything from "commissary" to "post office." The huge windowless sound stages dominated the movie studio, containing the interior sets where the actual filming took place. Each one had a large number painted in white over the entryway. She found Stage 10 easily enough, but saw that the red light over the door was flashing. A large red-lettered sign on the door warned visitors not to enter when the light was flashing because filming was in process. Luz waited, and in a few seconds the light stopped blinking. Once inside, she found herself momentarily blinded by the contrast between the bright sunlight outside and the dense darkness inside the cavernous building. The air smelled dank and stale, and it was extremely hot. In spite of the high ceilings, which were heavily crisscrossed with scaffolding and arc lights, she felt an odd, oppressive atmosphere about the place. Her eyes slowly adjusted to the gloom, and she walked carefully, avoiding the many cables and light stands that cluttered the place. So much for the glamour of Hollywood, she thought, almost tripping over the outstretched legs of a workman who seemed to be fast asleep on the cement floor. A bank of lights suddenly flared around a group clustered on a small set to the side, and she began to head in that direction, but she froze in her tracks when the high whine of a buzzer broke through the noisy racket of voices and the hammering on sets still being built. Someone made a great deal of noise shouting *"Quiet!"* and she stifled a laugh upon hearing that old movie cliché actually in usage. Standing as still as possible, she strained to watch what was taking place. "Rolling," the camera operator said. A pause, and then the soundman called, "Speed." Mario waited a split second, judging his actors, then said quietly but firmly, "Action." The set was a very elegantly furnished room, and Juanito was sitting on a sofa talking and gesturing to a sophisticated blond actress who was perched next to him. Luz couldn't catch any of the dialogue, for the pair were speaking almost in whispers. The "take" seemed to last only two or three minutes, then the hot quartz lights were switched off, and everybody in the group immediately relaxed. It was all very casual and very unemotional. She cautiously approached when she saw Juanito walk past the cameras and equipment encircling the set, but she hesitated when Mario came into view suddenly and stopped to talk to Juanito. With a few words and a small gesture, Mario apparently cleared up some bit of business easily, and Juanito nodded vigorously, paying close attention.

Strangely, and for the first time, she was struck by the physical similarity between the two of them. Why hadn't she noticed it before this instant? They were about the same height, both had the same slim build and dark hair, and even the dim light could not hide the fact that both were almost absurdly good-looking. But those same shadows sharply outlined and accentuated the differences in their mannerisms and personalities, too. Mario commanded attention even while standing still; Juanito was in constant motion. Mario walked and talked with the ease of experience, while Juanito was very much the eager pupil.

Somebody called out to Mario from the other side of the set, and he walked away after a last word with Juanito. It was then that Luz called out, "Juanito? Hi, I'm over here."

"*¿Cómo estás, hermana?*" Beaming, he sauntered over.

This was the first time Luz had been on the set, but she had been able to talk to Juanito in her office many times in the past weeks. She had deliberately avoided coming here, and since Juanito was more than anxious to visit her office, the script was practically finished. She laughed, as

102

usual, over his use of the familial *"hermana";* Juanito had decided if he couldn't be her lover, then he would appoint himself her surrogate brother.

"Hey, I was just talking to Mario. Let me call him," Juanito said after giving Luz a bear hug.

"No, don't call him. I mean—he looked very busy, and I don't want to disturb him," she finished rather lamely.

He gave her a fast look. "You two busted up, huh?"

"Nothing quite so dramatic, really." How could a relationship that had never really begun be "busted up"? She had not seen Mario often after that chance meeting by the fountain in the park. She had kept him at a distance on purpose. Why? She didn't know why; even after hours, days, and weeks of agony she still didn't know *why!* "Anyway, we've worked very closely on my script, and Mario has been more than generous with his advice—and with his time, too." But almost always in her office or over a casual lunch, she might have added. By choice, she had not returned to that lovely room.

"You're giving me a lot of jive, Luz. I don't fool easy." He took her arm and steered her out of the building. "I'm not in the next scene. Let's walk and talk."

Walking along the artificial little streets, Luz felt she could breathe again. "There's nothing to talk about, Juanito," she insisted.

"Oh, I think there's a lot to talk about, only you won't let it spill out. Just like Mario."

"What do you mean?" Her eyes narrowed.

"Like I mention your name lately, and he clams up real funny." He laughed his brash laugh. "Say, listen, I care about what happens to my two favorite people, understand? Now take yourself, for instance. At first I would look at you and I would think, *'Wow!,'* "you know what I mean? Then you came up with this crazy idea of doing a flick on my life, and I really got to know you and to like you." His natural drive couldn't be suppressed for long, however. "Don't get me wrong, Luz. I like you—but I still look at you and think, *'Wow!'*"

"You sure know how to make a girl feel grand, Juanito. Thanks." She meant every word, and to prove it she gave him a quick kiss right on the tip of his nose.

He grinned. "You've just earned yourself some ice cream." He strolled over to a vending machine, deposited some coins, and extracted two bars wrapped in tin foil. They munched on the ice cream sandwiches as they continued walking. "I've gotten to know Mario, too. He's worked hard to make me look good. Did you know my part's been rewritten, and I'm going to get third billing when this movie hits the screen?"

"Mario did tell me you were doing fantastic, but I didn't know they had expanded your role. How wonderful!"

"*They* expanded *nothing*. Mario just went to the producer and told him he himself was going to write extra lines for me. It was all Mario's doing."

Luz would have smiled at the obvious hero worship that Juanito felt for Mario, but she was also aware of the boy's sincerity. She could understand exactly how he felt. Mario was easy to like—and to love.

"See, that's why I think you and Mario . . ."

"Stop it! I meant it when I said I didn't want to talk about him."

If Juanito knew anything, he knew women. Luz's protest set him to thinking, and he decided to try a little reverse psychology. "Maybe you don't want to talk about him, but I know somebody who does." He let that ride for a moment.

Luz had heard him very clearly. Half wanting to listen to what he was about to say, and half refusing already to believe any gossip about Mario, she finished her ice cream with great deliberation—and said nothing.

"Rita has been visiting the set quite a lot lately, and not always with Chuck Harrison. At first I thought she was around because of me and our little thing," he said with brutal frankness, "but then I saw her really concentrating on Mario. Now I know she doesn't come a mile of being in your class, and yet . . . how much can a guy take, huh? Even a guy as choosy as Mario?"

Luz didn't flinch. She was too shocked. Concerning Rita, she could believe almost anything. But Mario? Mario! No wonder Rita had avoided all contact with Luz, refusing even to share rides back and forth to work. Since that afternoon at Mario's, they had not spoken one word to each other. She refused to show her hurt to Juanito, and refused also to comment on what he had just told her. Juanito's bit of news helped her make up her mind about one thing, however. "I came here today because I thought I needed a bit more material, but I think the script's fine as it stands." Her voice was perfectly controlled. "Will you walk me to my car?"

"Sure," Juanito nodded, suddenly feeling like a heel. "Sure."

They exchanged only small talk on the way out to where her car was parked. Although what he had said about Rita was true, he felt more and more rotten every step he took. What Luz was feeling he could only guess. But he had meant well. How was he to know it would come down like this?

When they reached the car, Luz opened the lock to the trunk with a steady hand, then reached inside and extracted a bulky envelope. "Will you please give this to Mario? Tell him I will make any changes he thinks are necessary, of course, but as far as I'm concerned, it's finished."

"That's all? There's nothing else you want to tell him?"

"No. Just tell him it's finished."

Next morning, Mickey was waiting for Luz. "I thought I was the only one who got to work with the chickens around here," she rasped, taking a look at her wristwatch.

105

"I have an important report I must get out today," Luz answered, "so I thought I'd come in early before Betsy comes in."

The two women exchanged a smile, but there was no malice in it. Betsy could be infuriating sometimes, but she was also lovable.

"I just stopped by to drop that off," Mickey said, pointing to a packet on Luz's desk.

"Is it my script?" Luz asked, sitting down. Her eyes burned, but she remembered not to rub them. Sleep would help.

"Yeah." Mickey, who was usually in a rush and never wasted time dilly-dallying or gossiping, pulled over a chair and sat down. "Nobody ever accused me of being subtle, so I'm going to lay it right out. You look like hell." She pinned Luz back with a stare. "Mario looks like hell, too."

"Does he?" Luz tried to keep the sarcasm out of her voice. "Am I supposed to feel sorry for him? If he chooses to knock himself out . . ." Why with Rita? Of all the women chasing him, why with *Rita?* She had never felt so betrayed in her life.

"You know, that's exactly what I tell him," Mickey snorted. "I keep harping at him that he can't work all day and half the night, too."

"Work?" This time Luz didn't try to keep the sarcasm out of her voice. "Work or play, it's none of my business anyway, Mickey."

"So, that's what's itching at you."

"Nothing's itching at me."

"Cut the garbage, Luz. You and Mario haven't fooled *me.* I've felt the vibes whenever you came to his office." She gave the desk a hard rap, shocking Luz out of her lethargy. "He hasn't had time to play, as you put it, because he has been working like a dog on that film. This is his first biggie, and he's under a lot of pressure, too—and don't you forget it. He's been carrying Juanito Jimenez on his back, helping him, coaching him, practically doing everything he can for that kid but wiping his nose for him." She angrily poked a finger at the script. "And he's spent hours and hours helping you with *that*. Sometimes he doesn't even go home at night. I know, because I've found him many a morning dead asleep on that fancy sofa in his office with papers and notes scattered all over him and the reading lamp still on." Her concern was so genuine that Luz could almost believe every word. "I'm worried about him." Now she was really angry. "I'm the last person who should be giving advice to the lovelorn. I've had more husbands than an alley cat has fleas, but I'm going to dish some out anyway."

"I know you mean well, Mickey," Luz interrupted vehemently, "but I don't want any more advice. Juanito tried to help, and he only made things worse!"

"Juanito Jimenez is a man," Mickey scoffed, relegating the whole sex to a subhuman level, "and men only think they know women. It's up to *you* to take some direct action. Mario needs lots of tender loving care right now— and because he's got this case on you, you're the gal to do it." She spoke plainly, but from the heart. "Instead of crying your pretty eyes out in your virginal bed tonight, grab up a bottle of wine, march right into his office, bolt the door, look him straight in the eye, and take off all your clothes!" Mickey stood up and almost knocked the chair over in her extreme exasperation. "And don't bother to bring glasses along for the wine, either," she growled, heading for the door. "It's ten times sexier when you just share it straight from the same bottle. And, Lord, you two need all the help you can get!" She was out the door like an explosion.

Luz was caught between wanting to laugh hysterically or uncontrollably sobbing her heart out. She did neither. Instead, she opened the packet and took out the script. Mario had included a hastily written note. She stared at it for a second, then read, "Minor changes marked. Otherwise, great job. J. gave me your message. Script, yes. Us, no."

She pushed aside the report that needed immediate attention and leafed through the script. Mario had indicated relatively few changes. Intently concentrating now, she picked up a pen and went to work revising the script. Less than an hour later, she was finished.

"G-o-o-d morning!" Betsy's arrival was as boisterous as usual. "I'm late again, aren't I?"

"It's all right," Luz sighed, taking a deep breath. Betsy bustled about getting herself prepared to settle down to work.

Luz looked over at the report, and then she looked down at her script. "Betsy, do you have lots of work piled up?"

"Well, yes and no." She made a face. "Why?"

"I want to ask you to do me a favor." Luz flicked the papers in her hand. "Could you type this script for me? I have this report I must get out today. I'll stay late tonight and finish up your work, too, if you can do this for me."

"That's a fair deal. Sure! I've been dying to read your script, anyway. Give!"

They exchanged papers from one desk to another. Just as Betsy poised to begin typing, she let out a big sneeze.

"Cold or allergy?" Luz asked with concern, watching Betsy swabbing away at her nose.

"Allergy! I'm doomed, I tell you. Everybody else can sniff flowers and enjoy their smell. Me? I just have to look at a clump of weeds, and my eyes get bloodshot and my nose looks like I fell into a can of red paint." She belabored her nose again.

They worked in relative peace and quiet for the rest of the morning and into the afternoon, but Betsy's sneezes grew louder and louder. Finally, Luz took pity on her. "You sound awful. Why don't you go home? This report

108

is almost finished, and I can get to your work soon. Go on, Betsy."

"I think I will." Another sneeze. "I'll finish your script first thing in the morning, okay?"

"Oh, don't worry about it." Luz felt guilty. "It was nice of you to tackle the typing. Thanks so much, and I promise to finish your work. Now please go home and get some rest."

After Betsy had left, Luz at last had a moment to think about what Mickey had said this morning. She thought about Mario falling asleep in his office and then glanced over at her script lying on Betsy's desk. Again she felt a wave of guilt. Then she remembered Juanito's sordid little story about Rita. About Rita and Mario. Who could she believe? More important—who did she *want* to believe? Luz balanced the knowledge of Rita's reckless behavior against the improbability of Mario having a fling or affair with Chuck Harrison's girl friend, and all she could come up with were the same doubts and ghosts that had been haunting her. The truth haunted her, too. She had knowingly driven Mario away, so his actions should be none of her concern. In spite of her own weaknesses, however, he had helped her with the script. She was dizzy from trying to figure out the truth. With a grim effort, she dove back into her work.

But driving home, her mind still whirled and swirled around the same puzzling questions. Then she decided she would probably become slightly unhinged if she kept thinking, and by the time she parked the car in front of her house she had resolved to pull herself together.

Trina greeted her with a warm kiss and a loving hug. "You worked late again tonight, didn't you? You look so tired. Have you been sleeping well at night?" She gazed at Luz intently.

"I always sleep like a log, you know that." Luz had gone out of her way not to wake her sister as she had paced in her room night after night. With luck, Trina would never know any of the details of this miserable mess she had gotten herself into. "How did it go today in the bakery?"

"Quite hectic." Trina smiled happily, however. "But business was good. Now sit down and we'll have supper. I have to rush because tonight is my night for the movies, you know."

"That's right! Well, let me help you so that you won't be late."

They had just finished eating before Luz remembered to ask, "Are you going to the movies with Maria Lopez?" Mrs. Lopez was Trina's closest friend, she lived right next door, and she was also a fellow film addict.

"No, she couldn't make it tonight. She was busy with some . . . family business."

"You're not going alone, are you?"

"No, I'm going with Mrs. Campos."

Luz was surprised. "Mrs. Campos? I didn't know she enjoyed going to see Spanish films. She's never gone before, has she?"

"No, but actually it was my idea that she go to the movies tonight."

"Why?" Luz knew Trina was being very secretive again, and she tensed.

"To take her mind off all her problems for a few hours, at least." She sniffed back the tears that suddenly filled her eyes. "Not only her problems, but also her disgrace!"

"What disgrace? Everybody knows Mrs. Campos is the most moral, pious person in the neighborhood. What happened?"

"Don't *you* know?" Trina wept. "Didn't your best friend tell you?"

Rita! Of course, Rita. "I haven't really seen very much of Rita lately." She didn't know what else she could possibly add to that.

"Well, Luz, thank God you've come to your senses. I told you that girl was a tramp. Just as I said to Jorge Garcia that night you and Rita were so rude to him . . ."

"I thought you told me Jorge had left very soon after we left? Not so soon that you didn't have time to talk about *me*, right?"

"We didn't *talk* about you, we *discussed* you—and your *friends!*"

"And I bet he couldn't wait to go home and tell my brother his nasty stories." Luz knew *one* story the old buzzard wouldn't dare tell her brother!

"I told your brother. I wrote him and told him everything."

"Trina, I . . ." But she couldn't be angry with Trina, not while the woman was sitting there with tears running down her kind face. "What happened with Mrs. Campos?"

"She was forced to throw Rita out of the house!" Her face twisted up in horror. "Imagine the pain! A mother being forced to disown her own daughter." Trina was openly crying now. "She wantonly boasted in her mother's face about—about . . . !"

Luz could well imagine what Trina couldn't bring herself to say. She could almost hear Rita's screams and visualize her demonic temper. She felt very sorry for Mrs. Campos. And for Rita. Where had she fled? There was only one place, one person. Chuck Harrison.

As Luz watched her sister tremble with sobs over the trials and pains of a neighbor, she stretched her hand to grasp hold of the quivering woman . . . and stopped. What right did she have to smugly pity Rita, Luz questioned herself? Was she herself any better than Rita? If it hadn't been for that grotesque interruption that night she would have freely and joyously given herself to Mario—again and again—that day, any day. She wanted him now, to-

111

night—right at this moment! No, she wasn't only smug; she was worse, she was a hypocrite. Trina's warm heart was breaking because a girl down the street was a tramp. What would it do to her sister if she knew that Luz . . . ?

"Trina, no!" She rushed to her sister and grasped her in her arms. "Please stop crying! You're so good. You've been so good to me."

Luz's strange outburst halted Trina's tears. "Why, what's the matter, dear? Oh, I know. You're upset about Rita, aren't you? Yes, I can understand," she sighed, stroking Luz's hair. "I can remember when you were both still little girls, and I would meet you at the convent after school and take you both shopping for a treat, or some little gift. Remember how you always insisted on wearing exactly the same color ribbons in your hair?" The memories were good for Trina, but they were tearing Luz apart.

She couldn't bear it anymore. "Trina, listen to me. That was a long time ago." But she couldn't go on; what would be the use? "I think you should think of helping Mrs. Campos now. She needs your support and your strength. It was a very good idea to think of inviting her to the movies." She continued even though the words were choking her. "Now hurry up, or you'll miss the beginning of the picture and you know how much you hate that."

"Yes, all right, dear," she replied, quickly taking off her ever-present apron. "I'll just wash my face a little and then I'll go."

Ten minutes later Trina left the house, intent on her mission of mercy, but still dabbing at her eyes with her handkerchief. The house was very quiet. Luz automatically began to clear the table, stacking the dishes very carefully on the drainboard. She had just placed her hands in the soapy dish water, when she heard the doorbell ring. Trina? Perhaps she had forgotten something.

When she opened the door and saw Rita standing there,

112

she felt a peculiar sense of inevitability. They remained static until Luz murmured, "You'd better come in."

Rita didn't appear agitated or nervous. It occurred to Luz that the calmness with which Rita walked into the house and then seated herself at the round kitchen table was an assumed and false stance. She knew this girl too well to be fooled any longer. "I'll put up some water and make you some tea." Rita had always liked *té de canela*, a thin, pungent brew of cinnamon sticks that always slightly nauseated Luz. Waiting for the water to boil, Luz set out the cup, spoon, napkin, and the required cream on the table in front of Rita. "Weren't you taking a big chance coming here? What if my sister had answered the door?"

"This is Wednesday, and Trina always goes to the movies on Wednesday nights. Funny, the things you remember," Rita answered cynically. "I waited outside in the car until I saw her leave."

"Waited for what? Why did you come here?"

"Maybe I got homesick for the old neighborhood." The retort was dripping with sarcasm. "After all, I haven't seen it for weeks."

"I didn't know you had left home until my sister told me tonight."

"Always the very proper Latina young lady, aren't you? I didn't 'leave,' I was ordered out of the house. My mother was deathly afraid I might contaminate my little sisters with my 'whoring ways.' I think that was the term she used. She could have used the word 'love,' but she was very angry." She cast her eyes around the neat little house, and then at the neatly and carefully set table that Luz had prepared for the tea. Then she gazed at Luz. Calm and cool. Luz looked lovely, with very little makeup, and so simply dressed. Rita nodded knowingly, and hissed, "Considering everything—which word would you have used, Luz?"

The tea kettle screeched, and Luz proceeded to methodically brew the cinnamon tea. "That would depend on whether you were sleeping with Chuck Harrison or Juanito Jimenez." She poured the hot tea with precise care into the china cup, careful not to scald Rita with a single drop. "With Chuck Harrison I would have said 'love,' since I think that's the term you used." She lowered the teapot slowly to the table before it scorched her fingers.

"And with Mario Maldonado—if I went to bed with him—then what word would you use?" Rita smoothed the cloth barely covering her thighs in a familiar, provocative motion, then reached for the cup and took a tiny sip. When her full pink lips left the pale china, a rose stain remained to mark the spot where her mouth had been.

"Bitch." Luz answered the question without inflection or emotion. For the first time she saw beneath Rita's hard, artificial beauty to the real core of the woman. She's vulgar, Luz realized, and a woman like this would disgust Mario, not attract him. "I would also add 'liar.'"

"You're right, Luz, but I sure as hell tried!" Her laugh was meant to be taunting, but it was only raw and pathetic. "I didn't have to try too hard with Juanito, though." She peeked up at Luz, surprised by her silence. "Ah, come on! Aren't you just a teeny weeny bit shocked about me and Juanito? Aren't you going to give me one of those l-o-n-g, dry, sincere lectures? Remember all that gooey moral stuff you were always spewing out? What happened? Have you changed your tune since the last time I saw you," she screamed, "when you were in that huge square bed, writhing, moaning, and half out of your mind, with Mario!"

If Luz had retaliated like she wanted to, she would have lost the struggle. Instead, their roles changed suddenly, and it was Rita who lost control. "You should be throwing something in my face for saying that! I don't believe *this*. Here I am, feeling lousy and rotten," she sobbed convulsively, "and you're standing there cool, calm, and *so damned superior!*"

Luz heard Rita's dreadful sobs and saw the tears running from her eyes smearing her makeup; and she turned away, feeling nothing at all. She was weary of comforting others—Rita, Trina, even Betsy. The only feeling left was the desire to crawl into Mario's arms and whisper to him precisely how much she loved him. In place of that fantasy, she prosaically helped herself to a cup of the abominable tea, knowing it would pass tastelessly through her mouth. She waited, drinking slowly, and watching Rita's rage drain away.

"I ran to Chuck after that scene with my mother," Rita gasped, illogically drifting into the genuine reason for her hysteria, "and I knew immediately I had made a mistake expecting him to welcome me ecstatically. Oh, he took me in, but he was annoyed and irritated. I found out soon enough why he didn't want me living with him." She covered her eyes with one hand. "I thought it wouldn't bother me—the other women, I mean—but it has. I pulled a lot of stupid stunts to make him jealous and to try and hold him. That's why I went around with Juanito for a while, but it didn't make any difference to Chuck . . . and that hurt!" She looked up at Luz with a fire in her eye that was almost staggering. "Maybe you and I don't love in the same way, but I'll do anything, *anything* to make him love *me!*"

"Can you force somebody to love you?" Luz wondered out loud.

"You can—when you know some of his weaknesses and secrets."

"That's blackmail, not love."

Rita shrugged. "If it gets me what I want, I don't care what it's called." She cast her eyes down swiftly, and Luz did not see the terrible change that took place—a shift from despair to desperate cunning. "Let me make you

115

some coffee; you hate that tea," Rita said, getting up suddenly and fussing with the coffeepot. "I owe you for a few things, so let me do this for you, okay?"

"You don't owe me anything," Luz murmured carefully, puzzled by Rita's swift change of emotions.

"Sure, I do—if for nothing else than just listening to my gripes. But I've been doing all the yakking. What about you, Luz?" She smiled brilliantly, shaking her head. "I don't mean about Mario. I mean about other things. Tell me what you've been doing—at work, for instance."

"You know all about my work, Rita. Nothing's changed."

"Well, I meant—your writing. Juanito just mentioned that you and Mario were writing a film, or something about Juanito's life."

"Oh, it's nothing that grand, and I don't think Mario would want his name associated with it. It's a small idea of mine, that's all."

"But Mario did help you with the script, and even wrote some of it, didn't he? And it's almost finished, isn't it?" Her voice was as light as her movements. The coffeepot was perking away, and Rita was actually smiling now.

So utterly relieved that Rita was willing to calm down and chat about something as unimportant and insignificant as the script, Luz let herself relax for the first time since Rita had walked into the house. "It's all written, and Betsy will finish typing it tomorrow morning."

"Tell me more about it. Sounds very interesting," Rita urged, pouring out a nice, large mug of coffee for Luz and serving it to her with a wide smile. "Come on, don't be shy."

Encouraged by Rita's prompting, Luz easily fell back on the habit of confiding and talking with Rita. She outlined the main points of the story, and the next hour was spent discussing the script in some detail. ". . . and so

116

that's it," Luz said, leaning back in her chair, while Rita refilled her cup.

"It sounds wonderful, Luz. Any plans for it?"

"No, none at all. Come on, Rita, it's only my first effort, and I'm nobody."

"But Mario Maldonado is certainly *somebody,* and he guided you." She waved her hand signifying a small point. "Chuck would love to have Mario write and direct something for him. Oh, I mean something Chuck could *produce.* But"—Rita wrinkled her nose, and shook the idea aside as being too complicated for her little brain—"that will never happen." She gave Luz a small hug. "Let's not talk about men, or we'll start arguing again. You haven't told any department head or producer about your script, have you?"

Luz laughed at that absurd idea. "Of course not!"

"Well, I'd love to read it, anyway. Why don't I stop by your office tomorrow morning, and I can take a look at it?"

"I'm sorry, but I have a meeting tomorrow morning and I won't be in my office."

"Well, how about if I come around later. I know! I'll treat you to lunch—and then I can read the script."

"The staff meeting usually goes right on through lunch-time. Let's make it another day for lunch, all right?" Without any reason, Luz experienced a faint unease, just a vague disquiet that she shook off quickly.

"Oh, fine," Rita agreed. She began to rattle off about all the new clothes Chuck had bought her, and went on to describe how expensive his new boat was, what with docking fees and everything. Another hour slipped by quite nicely. Rita happened to glance at her wristwatch. "I'd better take off before Trina gets home. It's been like old times, hasn't it, Luz."

"Yes. I'm glad we could talk, even for a little while."

"Have to run. Oh, Luz, for your own sake, don't bother

to tell anyone I was here, okay? Not even Mario, promise?"

"I promise." What difference would it make to Mario, Luz mused?

"We'll have lunch next week," Rita tossed over her shoulder as she left the house. "Don't forget. 'Bye!"

Luz walked back into the kitchen and cleaned up. She decided not to wait for Trina, and went straight to her bedroom as soon as she put the last dish away in the cupboard. She had quite forgotten her momentary uneasiness. She was numb with fatigue and too drained to think or feel. She was sound asleep the minute after her head hit the pillow.

The staff meeting dragged on and on. Luz had trouble paying attention to the business on hand, not because she was uninterested, but because she desperately wanted to call Mario. She wanted to thank him for helping her finish the script, and she was frankly intrigued by his message of "Us, no." That cryptic meaning had gone through her mind today again and again, especially after Rita's confession last night. At last, the meeting was brought to a close, and Luz almost ran all the way back to her office.

Betsy was nowhere around, but Luz immediately spotted the note atop her typewriter. "Allergy worse. Couldn't stick it out until you returned. No flowers at my funeral. *Please!*" Betsy had also scribbled the time she had written the note; it read 11:30. It was after one o'clock now. Luz wondered why the poor girl had bothered to drag herself in today at all. Was it possible she had done so only because of her promise to finish the script? Of course, that was it! Luz felt a gush of remorse, remembering the many times she had come pretty close to biting Betsy's head off. She glanced on either side of the typewriter looking for the script. Not finding it, she went around to her own desk. There was no sign of the script there, either. That's strange, Luz thought. She searched through Betsy's desk and then through her own desk. Nothing. Perhaps that foolish girl had taken it home in order to continue typing even though she was ill? Luz sat down at her desk and dialed Betsy's home phone number.

"Hello," came a very groggy-sounding voice over the line.

"Hello, Betsy. This is Luz. Oh, my, you sound awful!"

"I sound worse than I feel, actually." There was a sneeze, and then, "Well, say something! How do you like it?"

"Like what . . . ?"

"Your script, of course, silly. It's right there on your desk under the note I left for you."

"There's nothing here, Betsy. Are you sure you didn't take the script home by mistake?"

"Of course, I'm sure! I finished typing it this morning, and I took all your notes and the final draft and clipped everything together. I put the whole pile on your desk and left my note on top of it." Another sneeze, then, "Well, honestly, Luz, it *has* to be there. It just didn't get up and walk away, you know!"

"Hardly," Luz replied dryly, "but it seems one of us is going a little batty. I tell you, it's not here." She glanced at Betsy's note. "Another thing, I found your note on your typewriter and not on my desk. I guess somebody must have moved it. But why?"

"Ah-h-h, I bet your friend Rita Campos has something to do with this mystery."

"Rita?" Something flipped over in the pit of her stomach.

"Yeah, she came to take you to lunch, she said. I left her waiting for you when I came on home. She was very interested in the script. Well, I didn't think you'd mind—because she's your friend—so I just left everything there with her. I mean, it was okay to do that, wasn't it? Hey,

119

I'll bet she borrowed the script to read it. But I think she had a *nerve* to take it without asking your permission, don't you think?"

"Yes. Rita has nerve."

"Before I forget, Luz, I want to tell you that's one fine script! No wonder Mario kept urging you to finish it!"

"What? Oh, yes. Thanks, Betsy. Thanks for all your work, too."

"No problem. You did all my work, didn't you? Luz, are you still there? Luz?"

She hung up the phone while Betsy was still talking. If Betsy was correct, who else but Rita could have taken the script? Mario? But he would have left a note, surely. No, it had been Rita. But why? Why her sudden interest in this script? Why had she come to the office? Luz had clearly told Rita that lunch today would be out of the question. Yet, that's what Rita had told Betsy.

An insignificant script by an unknown, but partly written by *Mario Maldonado*. Another fact jumped out at Luz. Not only had the final draft been taken, but also all the notes and preliminary copies. Everything had been taken! But why?

Luz picked up the phone again. Chuck Harrison's office number rang unanswered. She found his home phone number on the executive's listings sheet, and dialed that number. No answer there, either. As she waited for each line to be answered and heard nothing but the insistent ringing, she kept recalling snatches of Rita's strange conversation last night. *". . . But Mario did help you with the script . . . Chuck would love to have Mario write something for him—but that will never happen . . . !"* Luz put down the phone finally, feeling little needles of coldness in her hands. What she was thinking just couldn't be possible. Too many people knew she had written that story. She could even take her complaint to the Writers' Guild. But why else had Rita insisted on knowing whether or not any department head or producer had been told about the script? The more she pondered the mystery, the more she became convinced Rita had taken the script, taken it for Chuck Harrison, because he had illusions of becoming a producer, and Rita had sworn, "I'll do anything, *anything* to make him love *me!*"

She was running down the hallways to Mario's office before she realized she should have called there, too. He probably was filming. Mickey looked flustered when Luz rushed through the doors of his office.

"Is Mario in?" Luz pleaded to know.

"No, he's not. Oh, my God! I forgot to tell you . . . !"

"Oh, he must be at the stage. Mickey, *please,* would you put through a call to him there?"

"I'm trying to tell you, Luz! He's in New York."

"New York? What is he doing there? When did he go?"

"I drove him to the airport this morning. I was supposed to tell you yesterday, but I got so wound up bawling you out that I forgot all about it!" All of a sudden, she didn't like the way Luz looked. "You sit right down there before you fall down." She urgently pushed Luz into a chair. Not knowing what was the matter, Mickey still realized it must be something awful, and she felt horrible about forgetting to give Luz Mario's message.

"Why is he in New York?" Luz kept insisting to know.

"Some of the story takes place in New York, and they're doing some location shots there. Only the second unit is shooting here."

Luz made a strong effort to control herself. What if the script's disappearance was just a stupid mistake? *No.* She knew it hadn't just been mislaid, or something equally as simple; not when Rita and Chuck Harrison were in the shadows. For herself she didn't care one iota, but Mario was involved. Mario and Chuck. She knew there was something hurtful and hateful operating between the two of them.

"How long will he be away, Mickey."

"A week." She saw the despair grip hold of Luz again. "I can try to reach him, or leave a message at his hotel. Luz, did you hear me?

"Yes, do that. Please tell him to call me. Just tell him to call me as soon as he can."

Luz was out of the chair and out of Mario's office before Mickey realized she still didn't know what was wrong.

CHAPTER SIX

Luz rushed to her car parked in the driveway. Only a basic stoic quality within her had stopped her from experiencing sheer panic in the past days while Mario had been in New York. It had taken almost two days to contact him since he had been rarely in his hotel. When Luz had finally received his call, she had almost crumbled from the relief of hearing his voice again. She had told him the whole story, from Rita's surprising visit at home to Betsy's account of what had occurred after she finished typing the script. His concern had been only for Luz. He would come home the moment the location shots were done, but meanwhile, she was *not* to attempt to contact either Chuck or Rita. He would take care of everything, he had promised. Luz was to do *nothing*.

Now—she would be meeting with him in less than an

hour and she could almost feel the presence of him and the strength of his arms around her. God, how much she needed the reassuring protection of those arms, and the sight of the unshakable calm of his face!

She quickly backed the car out onto the street and headed for the freeway, not on her way to the office but to have an early lunch with Mario. He had flown in this morning, and Mickey, acting as an efficient liaison officer, had taken care of all the details of where Mario and Luz would finally meet. The sun was bright and hot, and it pierced every corner of East Los Angeles. Luz noticed that it had become too hot for even the old men of the *barrio* to sit outside of the "Mom and Pop" grocery stores. The usually crowded central market was virtually deserted. The throngs of neighborhood housewives and their brightly dressed children had sensibly vanished indoors to escape the searing heat. Even the band of *mariachis* who serenaded in the market's courtyard during the late morning and noontime rush were silent and out of sight. Luz remembered many a Saturday afternoon spent at the market with Rita. Trina would take them along, and she would always reward them by buying fresh, crunchy *churros,* which had to be eaten immediately, before the dough hardened. She slowed down as she approached the school zone in front of the Convento de la Sagrada Familia. The schoolyard was empty. The nuns were keeping the young girls out of the blaze of the sun, probably in the confines of the cool, high-ceilinged library. She felt sadness again, recalling her vain attempt to induce Rita to apply herself to studying, especially when they had been cloistered inside that library during the long hours of a rainy-day schedule. Trina had been right; better to think of Rita in the past only.

She drove onto the freeway and the blast of heat off the asphalt was stifling. Moving swiftly from lane to lane, her mind was so preoccupied that she nearly missed the closest exit to Melrose Avenue, the street on which the famous Green Leaf restaurant was situated. Her head began to throb, and she suddenly had serious doubts about Mickey's choice of a meeting place. The Green Leaf was too chic, too much of a cachet for the rich "beautiful people," altogether too public; but it was also too late now to change plans. Luz spotted the green and white striped marquee of the restaurant and pulled sharply into the reserved parking lot.

She noticed in spite of her anxiety that the parking attendants did not give her the usual numbered ticket. The "smart" patrons were easily identified with their "smart" cars. She winced, realizing her own modest car would stick out like a sore thumb beside the other spectacular autos. A custom limousine nearly blocked the view of Mario's sports car, which took up a small space over by the side, but Luz's heart jumped with happiness knowing he had already arrived.

Once inside the gauze tent covering the patio, she hurried through the profusion of flowers to the desk of the host-owner.

"May I help you, mademoiselle?" His manner was exquisite.

"Mr. Maldonado's table, please." Why hadn't she insisted on meeting Mario somewhere else? Damn Mickey and her misguided attempt at romanticism!

At any other time Luz would have been overwhelmed with the beauty of this place, with its stunning decor of statues and indoor trees, but now she only strained to catch sight of Mario as she followed the host to a partly hidden table behind a superb terra-cotta fountain.

"Darling . . ."

"Mario . . . !"

They bent toward each other, but all they could do in this ridiculous public place was to clasp each other's hands.

"Mickey's brain must be getting soft in her old age," he muttered as soon as the host left. "Why the hell did we have to meet *here?*"

"She meant well," sighed Luz, gratefully sitting down and gazing at Mario across the table. She drank in the full force of him. Although he had traveled half the night he appeared completely rested and at ease. He looked calm, but when he brought her hand up to his mouth, kissing the tips of her fingers urgently, she could feel the tension and frustration through the touch of his lips. She sensed the tightness gripping his entire body; only his strong self-control was restraining some powerful surge of anger. She almost wished he would let go, even if it meant doing something utterly futile like banging his fist on the table. But she gazed deeply into those dark controlled eyes and knew it would never happen that way.

"Have you gotten any sleep?" she wanted to know, gently stroking the side of his face with her still-captured hand. Let people stare; she didn't care.

"No. I went for a swim instead. You wouldn't have liked it this morning, either. It was freezing cold. But it felt good." He reluctantly released her fingers and motioned to the waiter. "Another glass of white wine for me, please, and a Kir for the lady." He gave the man a further request. "I'll wait awhile before I order lunch." The waiter drifted away knowing he was *not* to intrude until he was openly summoned!

"You look beautiful to me, Luz."

"Ah, Mario, I don't feel beautiful! Until I saw you a moment ago, I've felt nothing but a terrible numbness."

"For a few moments, I don't want you to say one word about the script. I don't want you to do anything but look at me and listen to me. All that's happened has been my fault, anyway, but the worst thing I've done is to let you keep me at a distance." He frowned, and the expression constricted his angular, handsome face. "That's all over

125

now, darling. You're never going to be able to push me away again, do you understand?"

She couldn't answer. Whatever his terms, she would willingly accept. The only thing she really knew at this moment was that she needed him, she wanted him, and she loved him desperately.

The waiter brought their drinks to the table and then discreetly disappeared. Without knowing what she was doing, she sipped the Kir and shuddered when its full potency burned down her throat.

The teasing sparks flew back into his eyes. "Feel better now?"

Surprisingly, she did. "Yes—yes I . . . Yes, much better."

"Good. Take another sip," he ordered softly, "and then answer my question."

Again the powerful fluid flamed a trail through her lips and throat. She was aware of another of its effects; her head had stopped throbbing. Mario drank his wine and waited. She nodded her answer because she slowly grasped what his eyes were telling her: I love you!

"This isn't the place to . . ." he began, but stopped.

"I know."

They remained outwardly silent for a heartbeat or two, and then Mario broke the trance by signaling to the waiter.

"I'm not hungry." A strange obstruction inside was keeping her from breathing normally.

"Neither am I." He smiled that wonderful smile and reached for her hand again, clutching it fiercely tight. "But if I don't do something banal right now, like ordering lunch, I'm liable to do something I really want to do . . . !"

The waiter stood nearby, urbane and patient. Lovers caught up in a storm of awakened passion were nothing new to him. He took down Mario's distracted request for

". . . something light, maybe two salads . . ." and tried not to anticipate the touchy chef's howls of protest. He walked away with a correct smile on his face.

Mario's grasp became almost excruciating, but Luz didn't pull away. "I'm sorry, it's the last thing I want to talk about right now—but we can't ignore it any longer," he finally murmured. "Right from the beginning—tell me everything about the disappearance of that script."

Luz outlined every detail, every word of conversation, and then added her own thoughts. "Rita has done spiteful, harmful things in her life, but I can't believe she would do something like this to me," she finished.

"I can," he replied, "especially since she swore she would do anything for Chuck. I hate to say this, darling, but Rita was only following orders. The worst part of this whole business is that you had to take it alone. Chuck knew I was leaving for the east. He knew I'd be gone a whole week, too. He planned it perfectly, didn't he?"

"But *why*, Mario? Why didn't he just ask me for the script—or, why didn't he ask you?"

"Because he knew damned well I wouldn't allow him to have it!" He released her hand suddenly, aware he was hurting her, and merely folded her fingers within his. "We had a real blowout a few weeks ago because he insisted I write and direct a screenplay for him to produce. I told him exactly what he could do with his idea, and he didn't take it too well," he smiled, remembering. "I'll finish this picture, but I'll never work with him again. I don't like his methods, and I don't like the way he uses people. He's deeply in debt, he's in hot water at the studio, and he's desperate. He's also convinced his problems will be over if he gets his hands on a good script and"—Mario's voice was so low that Luz had difficulty hearing his next words—"he heard that your screenplay was great, so he just helped himself to it."

"But so many people know it was my story! Juanito, first of all, and Mickey, and even Betsy . . . !"

"My darling, you're going to have to be very realistic about this. In Hollywood, anything can happen. Ideas have been stolen and will be in the future, and there's not much that can be done about it. Just whisper a sentence or a word and somebody will grab it in an hour. The papers have been full of this sort of thing, and even the threat of bad publicity doesn't stop the pirating. But, Luz, if we have to, we can take *this* case to the Writers' Guild." He talked around the real problem very carefully, acutely worried that Luz would suddenly realize how vulnerable she was against a piece of scum like Chuck Harrison.

He almost slipped and let his relief show when the waiter brought their "light" salads. The salads were more than a distraction, however; they were incredible! Each frosted crystal boat was about a foot in diameter, and each held an assorted conglomeration of fruit so unusual and exotic that they could have only been reaped in some local garden of Eden. The waiter actually allowed a gleam of rather spiteful pleasure to escape his eyes before gliding away.

"I'm sure it will take us about an hour to even make a dent in these things," Mario remarked dryly, "so I suggest you start eating."

But once the sensation caused by the salads had somewhat abated, Luz's mind began whirling again. "How did Chuck first find out you and I were working on a script?" She absentmindedly played with her fork.

"Juanito told Rita." He concentrated on the first layer of fruit.

"But Juanito never read the script. How did Rita find out it was turning out well?"

He debated with himself for a long second, and decided to divulge the truth about the less upsetting of the two problems he was carrying around in his mind. "I told her." He paused in the middle of taking a bite and looked at her frankly. "Before you start jumping to any obvious conclusions concerning Rita and me, let me explain why she was on the set so much."

"Tell me, Mario." Her food remained untouched.

"It wasn't because of Juanito. That was over. She was there on the set to find out as much as she could, and in any way she could, about the script. She was there on Chuck's orders, Luz."

He watched as the blood drained away from her lips. "That's one of the most sickening things I've ever heard!"

He kept his eyes leveled directly at her. "She was your friend, so I just kept things going easily. I thought the script was a nice, general subject." He gave a dry, little laugh. "Either way, Rita has never appealed to me."

She shook her head, dazed. "It's so hard to believe all this about her. She was my best friend . . ."

"I once told you to forget about her. That still goes. Now come on, I want you to eat some of this stuff."

"I can't."

"Yes, you can. Darling, please."

Luz made the effort, speared a few pieces on her fork, and tasted.

"As far as Chuck is concerned, leave him to me. He's a loser. Believe me, none of his big-shot ideas will pan out."

"All right." She put some more of the fruit in her mouth, and this time she almost enjoyed it. What difference did that miserable script make, anyway? The only important thing in her life now was Mario. As long as none of this threatened him, she didn't care.

Slowly, as he talked to her about inconsequential, amusing things, her mood shifted and she found herself even laughing.

"By the way, Juanito has almost finished his role. He's done very well. I wouldn't be the least bit surprised if he goes on to have a major career." He smiled at the way she was making an effort to eat her meal. "He's very fond of you, you know."

"Maybe he likes me, but he absolutely worships you. Oh! Please don't let him know I told you that. He'd never forgive me," she pleaded.

"I wouldn't dream . . ." He cut his words short and remained looking over Luz's shoulder.

She turned in her chair and saw a man looming behind her. He was young and smiled at Mario in an almost too pleasant manner. He wore fancy sunglasses perched high in his curly blond hair and was dressed in casual denims, suggesting he was very much "in the business."

"Well, Mario, I'd never expect to see you having lunch in a place like this! This is much too establishment for you, isn't it?" Now his grin turned impudent. "Aren't you going to ask me to sit and join you?"

"Do I have a choice?" Mario waited until the impudent smile left the man's face, then casually motioned the waiter to bring up another chair. "Luz, this is Lenny Gannon." He noticeably did not turn the introduction around.

"Hello, Luz. You're beautiful—but then Mario Maldonado is *always* seen with *only* beautiful women."

Mario shrugged and finished his wine. Luz saw that dangerous sparkle of mischief leap into his eyes and knew that Lenny Gannon was probably in for a rough time. Lenny hitched his chair a little closer to Luz and confided, "Mario and I are friendly rivals, you know."

"Are you really?" She gave Lenny a vague smile, and then lifted her glass to her lips. Over the rim of the glass she shifted her gaze to Mario and pleaded for help. "Is that true, Mario?"

"No, not as far as I'm concerned. Oh, sure, Lenny carries a Directors' Guild membership card and he's directed a couple of 'hit' films, but then that doesn't automatically mean he's either my friend, or my rival." Now it was his turn to smile. "Will you have time for a drink, Lenny, or must you rush off?"

"Yeah, I have time." He leaned back and fixed Mario with a penetrating look. "I've had a very busy and exciting morning, so I guess I can spare the time to have a drink with you."

Mario ordered another round and left it up to Luz to fill the void. "Well, Lenny, if your morning was both busy *and* exciting, then you'll have to tell us all about it, won't you?" she quipped, shooting Mario a glare that he ignored.

Lenny rewarded her with one of his dynamite smiles, but his words were directed to Mario. "I think you'd be interested in a script my studio will probably buy especially for me to direct. It's right up your alley, Mario. You know, the kind of human interest thing you do so well."

Luz searched Lenny's face to see if he was being sarcastic, but she was startled to find that he seemed serious and sincere. Did she also catch just a touch of insecurity in his tone, as if he would be dealing with something a little beyond his scope?

Mario seemed intrigued all of a sudden. He waited until the drinks were served and then asked, "What do you mean by the kind of thing I do so well?"

"It's a kind of mood piece really, almost a documentary. Funny thing is, it's a subject you must know something about and frankly, I don't. The story follows a young Chicano's life in the *barrio* and then tries to explain what happens to this kid when he breaks out of his environment into a world that is sometimes hostile." Lenny was quite flattered by the intense silence that followed his brief explanation. He missed the stunned look on Luz's face. Wrapped up in his own flush of self-indulgence, he blundered on. "To tell you the truth, it's a natural for you, and I don't understand why Mercury didn't grab it for you to direct. It's all over town how great a job you're doing with your new film at the studio. Ah, well, I guess Mercury was just a day late and a dollar short, eh, Mario?" He tried for a levity that fell absolutely flat.

Mario risked murmuring aloud, "Luz, don't say anything . . ." but she deliberately cut right through his warning. "Is your studio negotiating to buy this script from Chuck Harrison?"

Lenny looked at Luz in bewilderment. "How did you know?"

"Did he tell you who wrote it?" she persisted.

"Of course! Chuck wrote it himself."

Mario twisted half out of his chair with a curse. "Are you sure Chuck said *he* wrote it?"

"Absolutely. There's no question about it! He even brought it around to my office and let me read it in advance. It's a great screenplay, let me tell you." He shook his head in surprise. "I never figured Chuck could write something like that, but he's come up with a winner." He took a large gulp from his glass and felt much better about a number of things. Some of his self-confidence returned. "Chuck's promised to deliver your discovery—what's the kid's name in your new picture? Juanito Jimenez, that's it. He promised me the Jimenez kid is in the bag for the lead." This time, even egotistical Lenny Gannon could not miss the turmoil his words had created. But if he had learned anything in this business, it was not to ask too many questions. Not when riding the crest of the high waves, you didn't. He hurriedly finished his drink. "Mario, I've got to run. Tough luck that you didn't get a shot at this, but better you than me, right?" What the hell was the matter with these two? "I'll be seeing you around. Hey, it was nice to meet you, Luz!"

How could Mario force himself to speak and act so normally, Luz wondered, as she saw him stand up with Lenny and heard him murmur a few illogical phrases like

". . . you'll do a good job, Lenny, don't worry . . ." and then ". . . good luck . . ."

"Mario . . . ?"

"Take it easy, Luz," Mario whispered as soon as Lenny had gone bearing a very puzzled look on his face.

"Stop being so protective, will you?" she cried. "I'm angry! I'm going to find Chuck, and I'll tell him exactly what I think of him. I'll tell everybody at Mercury what he's done to us!"

"Luz, darling, please sit down and let me explain something to you," he half-pleaded, grabbing Luz rather roughly by the arm and forcing her back into her chair. The urbane waiter was casting a sour eye in their direction. But Luz wouldn't sit still, and before Mario could stop her, she wriggled free of his hold and was running across the elegant restaurant. Mario slammed a large bill down on the table and ran after her.

He caught up with her just as she was sliding behind the wheel of her car. With one arm he reached for her and lifted her out, slamming the door shut behind her. "Are you going to listen to me?" he shouted, giving her a good shake.

"No! Let me go!" But she was stunned. She had never heard him shout before.

"If you go charging into Chuck, you're going to do yourself a lot of harm, believe me!"

"I don't care about myself, Mario. How can he harm me, anyway? He might hurt you—and your career at the studio . . . !" She slipped out of his arms the moment she felt he had loosened his hold and swiftly got back into the car. The motor revved, but Mario leaned in through the window and quickly shut off the ignition and removed the key.

"You have to trust me," he said with anger now, "because I know Chuck and you don't. This isn't some silly ego trip, Luz. This is a little more serious."

She rested her head against the wheel and some of her common sense returned after digesting Mario's words. He walked around, opened the door, and sat down in the passenger's seat. She could tell he was still fuming and chanced a glance in his direction. "I'm sorry. That was a stupid act I pulled in there," she said, nodding toward the restaurant. "It's just that I'm so frustrated about this whole thing. What hurts the most is Juanito being part of this awful plot. I don't believe he could do this to *you.*"

"I'll wait until Juanito tells me himself."

She twisted to face him. "What are we going to do?"

"*We're* not going to do anything. I'll find Chuck, and I'll take care of it. *No,* Luz," he snapped as she began to protest. "I want you to go directly home. Wait there until I get in touch with you."

She couldn't insist any longer, not when he looked at her with such fire. His sudden grip on her arm demanded her immediate attention and obedience. "Are you going to do what I tell you?"

She nodded. "Yes." But there was one promise she needed from him. "If you see Rita, please don't be too harsh with her."

He was surprised. "I can't figure you out. One moment you're out for blood, and the next moment you're ready to forgive."

"I didn't say I was forgiving her. I can't blame her for all that's happened, either."

"I understand." He bent toward her, but she had already pulled herself into his arms. "I want you to be happy, Luz," he whispered after he kissed her, "but now I'm asking you to go home." He gave her back her key. "Go home, and stay there until you hear from me."

The thought never entered Mario's mind that Chuck Harrison might be keeping a low profile and would make himself scarce. Mario knew Chuck too well. He would be very much in evidence, crowing, bragging, and openly gloating. Mario drove directly to Mercury, fully expecting to find Chuck holding court there, and that's exactly where he found him. Only, he was alone now. It was clear there had been a crowd in Chuck's office a few minutes before, because coffee cups littered the place and ashtrays were filled with crushed cigarette stubs. Mario closed the door with a care that gave lie to his inner rage. Chuck looked up beaming, obviously still basking in the glow of some deep satisfaction. When he saw Mario, he remained distinctly unperturbed. In fact, he added smugness to his grin.

"Where's Rita?"

Chuck's grin got bigger. "I sent her off to Las Vegas to have a little fun, see some shows, gamble a little, you know. She deserves it. She's earned it."

"Are you sure you can afford it?"

"Now I can," Chuck boasted. "Anyway, compared to other gals I've known, Rita doesn't cramp my wallet, just my style."

"You don't have any style, Harrison." Mario walked across to the windows, gazed outside for a beat, and then turned back to face Chuck. "When do you expect her back?"

"When I call her back, and not a moment before. Who knows? Maybe I'll never call her back. Why the sudden interest in Rita, Mario? You had your chance. What's happened, have you changed your mind?"

"No, I never lower my standards." Mario's voice grew quite soft. "I promised Luz I'd go easy on you if Rita was around." The tiny spark of wariness that crept into Chuck's eyes gave Mario a pleasant sensation deep inside and he hated himself for it. "Luz has quaint, old-fashioned ideas. She's honest, and she'll try to forgive somebody who has wronged her." He walked slowly in Chuck's direction. "But you know her virtues, don't you?"

"Oh, I know all about Miss Luz Rivas. Actually, Mario, I think you'd be surprised just how much I know about her."

"And still, you stole her script."

"That's right."

Mario sat down very comfortably on the far corner of Chuck's desk. "And you put your name on it, and you peddled it to another studio."

"Right again, my friend."

Mario's voice didn't change, but the next words hurt him deep in the gut. "You even swindled Juanito over to your side. How did you work that out?"

"Juanito's a hungry kid," Chuck sneered with contempt. "Real hungry. You remember how that feels, don't you, Mario? Before you could afford the sports cars, and the expensive clothes, and the gals from *this side* of town that cost you a wad? When you were young, and nobody gave a damn about you? You had nothing going for you but your own nerve and your own drive." He was smooth as oil. "Then somebody gave you a break, and you grabbed it, buddy! And don't give me any crap about reading the fine print, either. You came from nothing, Mario. You came from the fringe—from the *barrios* of East L.A. To get as far as you've come, you've had to step over a lot of bodies!" His expression was more demeaning than what he was saying. "Naw, the easiest part of the whole thing was getting Juanito. He came dirt cheap!"

Mario's built-in warning system held him back; not now, not *yet!* "How the hell did you think you'd get away with it?"

"You're a little mixed up, Mario. I *have* gotten away with it, and there's not a damned thing you can do about it!"

"Too many people knew Luz wrote that script," Mario remarked, almost too casually; Chuck should have been warned. "But, of course, you've taken that into consideration also, haven't you?"

"I sure have. You know how Luz has that little-girl quality about her that makes people want to protect her. The poor kid lost her *mamacita* and *papacito,* she's from the wrong side of town, and she's so worried about her reputation—and so are la señorita Rivas's friends!" Chuck leaned back in his chair expansively. "Come on, Mario, no more protests? Aren't you going to threaten me a little bit? Aren't you going to threaten to drag me to face a grievance committee of the Writers' Guild?" He threw his arms up in a mock gesture of surrender. "You'd win the case easily, you know."

"I know. And there wouldn't be a writer, director, or actor who would ever work with you again."

"I'd be ruined! They'd blacklist me in every studio in this town."

"You're tempting me," Mario murmured, and then smiled.

"You're bluffing, Maldonado! We both know it. You won't do a thing to me because you know I'll turn Rita loose." Chuck stood up and sauntered around to the other side of the desk, enjoying every inch of his victory.

"And she'll tell Luz's family about me." Mario finished wording the threat.

"Oh, not only Luz's family, but the whole neighborhood. And she won't be vague or subtle." His chuckle was dirtier than any four-letter word. "Can you picture it? A sister who is an old spinster and spends most of her time in church—a sister who is a paragon in the *barrio,* and who owns a neighborhood business. And a brother who is a priest! Everybody *thinks* little Luz is so pure and innocent. But Rita and me, we know firsthand that's not quite true. Yeah, we both know that demure little Luz has had her moments, eh?" He threw his head back and roared. "It's perfect!"

137

"Except that it needs the element of surprise to work," Mario replied provocatively, "and your filthy little story won't have that going for it."

Chuck's eyes crackled with suspicion first, and then confusion. "What are you talking about?"

"I'm talking about a lot of old-fashioned ideas you don't know anything about. Love and respect, and a number of other quaint traditions maybe you never had in *your* background." Mario had been sitting on the desk, but now he stood up, too. "When I leave this place I'm heading directly to Luz's house, and I will tell her sister exactly how I feel about Luz. If necessary, I'll take a fast flight down to Mexico and tell her brother, too. But—that will be after I file a case against you at the Writers' Guild. You were right about one thing, though. I *am* going to ruin you."

Chuck didn't back away, but he did shift his weight slightly in a very cautious move. He eyed the distance between himself and Mario carefully.

Mario didn't have to be cautious; he was functioning by sheer instinct now. "But before I do anything else, Harrison, I'm going to take you apart, piece by piece, and very painfully."

"Don't be an ass. I've got a thirty-pound advantage over you!" Chuck hissed out.

"Where I came from, thirty pounds meant nothing. Have you forgotten so soon—where I came from, I mean? There in the *barrio,* you learn to use anger, frustration, and hate as an advantage over heft. I thought I had left all that bitterness back there, but you've just made me realize I haven't. I've been carrying that hate around for years, like a chip on my shoulder. It's going to feel good to get rid of it," he whispered, deadly coiled, angry and dangerous now, "once and for all . . . !"

He smashed Chuck's head back with a release almost beyond mere physical satisfaction. Again and again he hit him until Chuck, doubled over and moaning with pain, fell limply to the floor.

"If you get up, I'll knock you down again," Mario promised, finding it very hard to breathe and talk, "and every time you get up, I'll knock you down again . . . !"

Chuck groaned and rolled onto his side. "You're—crazy!" He choked, gagged, and fought to bring air into his lungs. "You've just thrown everything away! And—for what! That little piece has taken you for a ride," he coughed out, getting as far as balancing himself on one knee. "She conned you so you'd help her write that script—that's all! *You're* the only one who doesn't know. She's all set to marry some fat old rancher from Mexico." He staggered to his feet. "And it's been going on for years, hot and heavy! Everybody knows. *Everybody but you* . . . !"

Mario felt no satisfaction at all when he slammed his fist into Chuck for the last time. All the anger and hate burned and scorched inward. He left and never glanced back.

CHAPTER SEVEN

The adrenaline had stopped flowing, and his pulse had almost returned to normal. Now that it was over, Mario felt the heat draining from his body. He didn't know he had punched the elevator button and had descended to the lobby until he found himself in the parking lot. The late afternoon sun had turned the day into a furious combination of sultriness and haze, and the underground garage, lacking air, was like an oven ready for broiling. He unlocked the car's door, and rolled down the windows; unable to force himself into the stifling airlessness of the vehicle, he shoved the door shut again. Turning restlessly toward the garage entrance, he walked to the front of the building, stopping finally to prop one leg up on the concrete ledge that bordered the trim lawn, and leaned his arms across his knee. He had hurt Chuck badly, he now realized, but he had to shut Chuck's lying mouth, permanently and forever.

"G'd afternoon, Mr. Maldonado. If you're trying to get a breath of fresh air, you'd better drive down to San Diego," jested the building's gardener-philosopher, sidling up to Mario with a grin that exposed nearly toothless gums. "It's so hot the birdies are falling out of the trees."

"Yeah, it's hot," Mario grinned back a little. "Must be tough working out here in this ooze." *Chuck;* no, he wasn't important, but what was it he had spit out about Luz? Luz, and some guy from Mexico?

"Ah, I've gotten used to it after so many years," the gardener replied with a wink. "And then, life does have its little rewards, doesn't it?"

"Does it?" Mario's voice was dry and bitter. His fists hurt, and he flexed them open and shut.

"Sure it does! Say, you know what's the matter with you young fellas today? You're too serious and too"—he searched his gray head for the right word—"and too 'motivated,' that's it. All you career types who work in places like this"—he nodded toward the Mercury building —"are all the same. You forget to enjoy the little things, the good little things, eh?" He screwed his face up into what looked to Mario to be the old man's idea of a pornographic smirk. "Now me, I'm goin' to go pick up m'gal after work, and have a real picnic up in the last row of the

140

Hollywood Bowl tonight." He hooted at his own idea of a joke. "Ever been to the Bowl, up there in the Hollywood hills, Mr. Maldonado?"

"A few times," Mario answered indistinctly, his mind still on Luz, and on what Chuck had said about her and some man.

"Bet you just went there, sat and listened to that classy music, huh?"

"Yeah, that's right."

"Well, that's where you made your mistake! Don't you know any nice young juicy gals?"

"What?" asked Mario, actually hearing only about every other word the old man was gibbering out.

"A good-lookin' healthy young fella like you should grab yourself a woman and go up there to the last row and do some hot smoochin', like me. Keeps me young and happy. It'll do you good!" He hesitated, again searching for the right term. "The kids today call it 'makin' out'!"

After a few moments, Mario regarded the old man with a kindly smile. "You know, you might be right. Thanks for the advice."

"It's free," the gardener chuckled, returning to his work after waving to Mario.

With Chuck's words persistently clinging to his mind, Mario walked quickly back to his car. When he stepped on the starter, the superbly engineered machine responded and purred to his touch, and the sound calmed him, somehow. After turning the air conditioning to maximum, he roared out of the garage and headed toward East L.A.

The shaded hills of the *barrio* had cooled faster than the rest of the basin now that the sun had begun to set. A car such as Mario's was not usually seen in this part of the city, and the neighbors stretched their necks over the front-yard fences to get a better look when he turned down Luz's block. He parked the car right in front of her house and locked it up without haste, allowing the neighbors to get a good look at him, too. He also took his time walking to the front door. He jabbed at the doorbell twice.

It was Trina who opened the door. She didn't recognize him; it had been very dark in the yard that night, many weeks ago.

"*¿Sí?*"

Hesitating, Mario suddenly thought—how was he to address Trina? *Señora* was out of the question since she had never been married. At her age, *señorita* would seem awkward. He knew these little items of protocol could sometimes make or break a relationship right from the start, so he opted for the easy way out, using neither. "*Buenas tardes, me llamo* Mario Maldonado. *¿Está en casa* Luz?"

The bells from a nearby church began to peal just as he stopped speaking, and he congratulated himself for luckily remembering the correct term for the time of day. For an Hispanic, it remained "afternoon" until the bells called for vespers regardless of where the sun happened to be in the sky.

He would need every stroke of luck he could get. Trina had recognized his name, and her face immediately froze into a mask. She opened her mouth to say something, but quickly seemed to change her mind and remained at the door, silent.

"Mario?" He heard Luz cry out his name from somewhere in the house. "Mario!"

Luz appeared to stand next to her sister. Because Trina refused to either welcome Mario or move out of the doorway, she was forced to reach around Trina's shoulders and fling the door open all the way. "Mario, please come in."

"*¿Con permiso?*" he responded politely, and receiving a stiff, reluctant nod from Trina, entered the house. He was very aware of the many questions leaping out to him from Luz's beautiful eyes, but both of them knew that proper

142

introductions must come before anything else. Trina shut the door and waited.

"Mario, I want you to meet my sister, Trina Rivas."

Fine! Mario thought, now he would really be put to the test, and made a fierce effort to address this forbidding-looking woman correctly. He remembered just in time. *"Mucho gusto,* Doña Trina."

Mario well knew that now it was Trina Rivas's turn to show good manners and welcome him to her house. He waited, tensely, not for himself, but for Luz.

A hint of surprising approval appeared in Trina's eyes for a moment, but was completely erased almost immediately. Her words were spoken in the same stiff manner as the way she held her back and her head when she murmured, *"Esta usted en su casa, señor."*

Mario clearly heard Luz's sigh of relief, although Trina looked as if she had just been forced to commit an unpardonable sin.

"Trina, it's very important that I talk to Mario," Luz explained. "Would you please get him something to drink while we talk?"

"Coffee, Mr. Maldonado?" It was more of a statement than a question.

The last thing Mario wanted was anything hot to drink, but he quickly answered, "Yes, thank you."

Trina left for the kitchen. Luz pulled him into the living room, and then she spun around immediately to ask, "Did you find Chuck?"

"Yes, he was at the studio."

"Please, tell me what happened. You look awful." In her anxiousness, she grasped his arms and clung to him.

"Let's just say we struck a bargain." His arms involuntarily moved to hold her closer even though there were questions he had to ask her. "But I don't know if Chuck will keep his end of the bargain."

"A bargain? I don't understand. He admitted stealing

143

my script and trying to sell it under his own name, didn't he?"

"Oh, yes, he didn't bother to deny that at all."

"Did you tell him you would bring it to the attention of the Guild?"

Mario nodded, but he knew that he wouldn't be able to keep up this pretense much longer. Not while she was pressing herself so hard against him—not while Chuck's choking taunts still stung his mind. "Luz, have you ever told your sister I was helping you write a script?"

"Yes, in a very general way. I haven't told her anything about Rita stealing it, though. It would only upset Trina." She pulled her head back a little.

"Have you told her anything about us?"

"Why, Mario?"

"Chuck felt safe." There was no other way; he had to tell her. "He threatened to tell Trina about us, about that night in my apartment, if we spelled out the truth to anybody."

She trembled and gasped. Mario gathered her to him and he heard her whisper, "I knew it. I remember the look on Rita's face."

"I had hoped you had forgotten." But now he knew Luz had never told her sister about him, either. Why not?

It was cool and quite dark in the room. The evening's shadows had settled, and they could not see each other clearly. Luz pulled away and turned on one of the lamps in the room. "Will she tell my sister?"

"No, that's no longer a threat. I told Chuck I would tell Trina myself."

Luz looked at him in disbelief. "Tell Trina! *You* would tell her?"

"I would tell her that I love you, and that I want to marry you."

She took a step, and then another step. Why were they standing so far apart from one another? She had waited so long to hear him say exactly those words, and yet he didn't move to hold her. "I love you so very much," she murmured. "I have for such a long time."

"As much and as long as you've loved that rancher from Mexico?"

"What?" They were both whispering, and Luz knew she must have misunderstood. "What rancher . . . ?"

"The one you may have been planning to marry. What's his name, Luz?"

He had never seen somebody actually cease to breathe. Seconds ticked by as the clock on the table kept perfect time with the blood pulsating through his veins. He was giving her only one more second to deny it.

"His name is Jorge Garcia," he heard a voice say, a voice that wasn't Luz's.

Trina carried the coffee cup to the side table. "Luz has known him for years. Jorge is a dear friend of our family, and his most fervent desire is to marry her. Of course, my brother and I wish for no greater joy than to bless their union." She turned to face Luz. Her smile was a strange mixture of warmth and triumph. "I'm surprised you haven't told Mr. Maldonado about Jorge, dear."

Luz veered ever so slightly to gaze at her sister. "I didn't tell Mario about Jorge Garcia because there is nothing to say." She was too angry to shout, or cry, or strike her sister, something she had actually thought of doing a second ago. "Jorge Garcia has been asking me to marry him for eight years because you've instigated him to keep asking me. For eight years I have been saying 'no' to him. I will continue to say 'no' to him for the next *eighty* years, if necessary. I hate him!" She looked at Mario, but she refused to beg. "If Chuck told you about Jorge, then he must have only been repeating Rita's lies."

"You know how much it hurts me to hear you say that, Luz!" Trina dug into her apron pocket and took out a letter. She laid it flat on the same table on which she had

145

placed Mario's coffee that was still there, untouched. "I received this letter from your brother yesterday." Trina stepped away from the table, but nodded toward the letter. "He writes that he is so concerned about your future that he has made plans to come to Los Angeles." She went right on talking as if Mario was not there. "He might be thinking that I haven't been a very good mother to you. Perhaps he's right."

"*He* won't change my mind, just the way *you* haven't been able to change my mind for eight years. I hate Jorge Garcia," Luz sobbed, her voice cracking for the first time, "and I love you, Mario. Do you believe me?"

Luz swore to herself that if Mario didn't say something, say *anything,* she would run from this room and run from this house. She had lived through a week of hell. No. She had lived through *weeks* of hell; she had no strength left. Her best friend had betrayed her, and now her own sister was tormenting her in front of the man she loved. And Mario? Why didn't he answer?

Mario's insight told him not to pressure Luz at this moment, not while Trina was standing there. A matter of pride was involved on all sides, Hispanic pride, the strongest of all impulses. Chuck had not even come close to guessing that this struggle between Luz and Trina, with himself caught in the center as catalyst, would prove to be the true crisis. But Mario knew; he had always known. "Luz, of course I believe you," he said, coming up to her and gently taking hold of her shoulders, "and I understand what's operating here."

Her elation broke through. "Mario . . . darling!"

"Luz!" Trina's cry of outrage tore apart the spell holding Mario and Luz. "My sister seems to have lost all sense of propriety. Mr. Maldonado, I think you should leave now."

"My name is Mario," he said to Trina. "It's as easy to say as 'Jorge,' or any other Latino name. Get used to saying it, Doña Trina." He watched with satisfaction as Trina's expression changed from wrath to outright astonishment. "And I will be leaving in a second."

"No! If you leave—I'll go with you!" Luz impetuously promised, and she clung to him fiercely.

"Sh-h-h, Luz," he whispered. With a tender yet firm push, he set her back away from him. "I don't want you to come away with me while you're angry and bitter. We'd be starting all wrong, and I want everything to be perfect for us. Please think this over very carefully. If you decide . . ." He stopped and rid himself of that improbability. *"When* you decide—I'll be waiting for you." His fingers lightly halted whatever hasty words might have escaped from her lips. "Good night."

Mario left. The two women remained in the room unable to look at each other, each fighting to suppress her own strong emotions. It was Trina who had the will to move first, and she picked up the letter from the table, folded it neatly, and put it back in her pocket. Next, she removed the cold cup of coffee. Holding it in her hands uncertainly, she then turned and marched off to the kitchen.

An overwhelming need to talk to somebody overcame Luz. Not her sister; *no,* not tonight, perhaps never again. Every inch of her mind and soul yearned to tell someone who would understand how terribly divided she felt at this moment. She needed badly to sit and talk and even cry, if necessary. Going quickly to her room, she took off the pretty paisley dress she had worn to the restaurant and changed into jeans and a sweater. She whisked a brush swiftly through her hair, snatched up her purse, and ran to the front door.

"Where are you going?" Trina called out after her.

"Not to Mario, don't worry," Luz said, deliberately keeping her voice steady and calm. "I won't be home late."

* * *

The graceful courtyard centered around a Moorish fountain jetting high streams of water. It made music in the night air. Luz glanced at the numbers of each of the scenic bungalows ringing the courtyard and walked over to the last one facing this colorful, outdated oasis. The doorbell didn't ring; instead, it chimed.

"Just a moment," the rough voice called out. "I'll be right there!" Luz heard some rattling as the door bolt was drawn back. "Well, for goodness' sake . . . Luz!"

"I'm sorry, but I just had to talk to somebody."

"Don't just stand there, come on in," Mickey rasped in her unique way, practically dragging Luz into the house. "Boy! I'm glad to see you." She took a better look at Luz's face. "Or, am I?"

"I hope I'm not disturbing you?"

"Hah, that's a laugh. The only thing you disturbed was a snore. I'd fallen asleep in front of the television set—*again.*" A second later she had thrown her arms around the girl and was hugging her to her skinny breast. Mickey had seen wet kittens that looked less pathetic than Luz did right now. Leading her trembling guest over to a large brocaded loveseat, Mickey growled, "Sit." With a low, rumbling curse, she then switched off the television and came paddling back on fluffy orange-slippered feet to plop down next to Luz. Finally, she shoved a box of facial tissues into Luz's hands. "Now *cry.*"

"What?"

"I said cry."

"Why?"

"Because if you don't, you're going to blow a fuse." Mickey nodded her head knowingly. "It's Mario, isn't it?"

"It's Mario, and my sister, and the script, and Rita, too. I've never been so unhappy in my life . . . never in my life . . ."

Luz fought hard to hang on to her self-control, but as

148

Mickey suspected, the battle was bound to be lost. Luz quickly covered her face with her hands, but the tears filtered through her fingers, and the haunting sobs brought tears gushing up into Mickey's own cynical eyes. It went on and on because it was a despair that had festered much too long within her in silence and frustration. Mickey stroked Luz's hair back from her face, and muttered every little soothing word she could remember. And still Luz cried. Now Mickey was getting worried. "Hon, don't. Nothing is worth this much misery." The tears had been cried out, but the sobbing continued. Finally Luz gasped and was silent.

"Okay, hon? Are you okay?"

Luz slowly nodded. Mickey hurried to slosh some brandy into two tumblers and held one out to Luz. Still silent, with the tears glistening on her face, Luz drank some of the brandy and then leaned back and closed her eyes.

Mickey snickered and shook her head. "I have to hand it to you, Luz. You've just spilled your innards out, and you still look gorgeous. All I have to do is sniffle once, and half my face falls on the floor. Some girls have all the luck!"

It did bring a tiny dry laugh out of Luz. "Some luck, huh?"

"You have a few other things going for you, or Mario wouldn't love you so much."

Luz opened her eyes all the way. "Mickey, what has he said to you about me?" Just like every woman who loved, she wanted to know every word, every secret, *everything* that concerned Mario.

"He lets that steel guard down once in a while. Mostly when he's tired. That's the only time he really opens up. He's crazy about you, Luz. Crazy like only a guy can be when he's seen it all, like Mario, and has finally met that

149

special woman. He's also a very special kind of person, you know."

"Yes, I know," Luz sighed, using the tissues to rub away the tears. "That's why I love him so much."

"Okay, he loves you and you love him. So, why are you so darned miserable?"

"Because Mario and Trina tangled tonight, and I was right there in the middle, trapped."

"Divided loyalties, eh?"

"Yes, I guess that's it." A dry sob racked her body. "He didn't say much about what happened today with Chuck. All he would tell me was that they struck some kind of bargain."

"Well, yeah—that's a very delicate way of putting it."

"What do you mean?" Luz sat up. "Do you know what really happened this afternoon. God! Mickey, please tell me!"

"Mario finally lost his temper and cleaned up the floor with Chuck." She shook her head. "Don't feel sorry for him, Luz. Chuck deserved whatever he got, the snake! Anyway, it's the talk of the studio, and by now everybody in town knows Chuck and Rita stole your script. It's probably all over for both of them at Mercury, or any other studio."

"Mario might have been hurt!"

"Now don't start bawling all over again! Don't forget that Mario probably learned to use his fists in the cradle."

"Ah, Mickey!" Luz suddenly jumped up and began to look desperate again. "What am I going to do?"

"You mean, how are you going to settle this thing between Mario and your sister?"

"That's exactly what I mean. I love him and I want to be with him. I would have walked out of my sister's house tonight with him—except he wouldn't let me. He said I had to decide."

"He's perfectly right, Luz, and the sooner the better.

But you'd be the world's biggest dummy if you lose Mario because you'd allow your sister to . . ." Mickey clamped her mouth shut, and shrugged.

"Go on, tell me what you're thinking."

"Straight from the shoulder?"

"Yes, Mickey, and I mean it."

"From the little I know, your sister suffered a lot to bring you up to be the beautiful person you are. Okay, but nobody forced her. She did it willingly and now it's over. What does she expect as her reward? Are you going to allow her to dominate you the rest of your life?"

"Dominate me? You're wrong, Mickey, I can do anything . . ."

"Can you?" asked Mickey, bluntly. "You can't even marry the guy you love without starting a revolution. Think about it."

"She only wants me to be happy."

"Like she's been happy?" Mickey took a good taste of the brandy. "Everybody has different ideas about 'happiness.'" She held her glass up and waved it in a mocking salute to her surroundings. "I'm very happy living here, for instance. Take a good look around, Luz."

The place seemed very comfortable. There was a fireplace in the corner, and a jumble of furniture all over the place. Luz had been so wrapped up in her own gloom when she had burst in that she had noticed little else. Now she wandered across the room, taking note of details and inspecting the house with a critical eye. Everything was slightly frayed and faded, from the slipcovers to the photographs of personalities who had been famous in Hollywood's past. The place was not unkempt, but the mustiness and cobwebs were hiding just around the corner, waiting to take over.

"Kind of creepy, isn't it? Every bungalow in this court looks about the same, and so do the people. I've lived here twenty-five years, but I'll have to move soon because the whole place will be torn down and replaced with condominiums. We're only a few blocks below the Strip and we've become obsolete, like the dinosaurs." She let out a snort. "So your sister spent her life working in a bakery, and I've spent my life working in a studio. Same difference, isn't it? Oh, yeah, I've had husbands walking in and out, but I've always lived here alone, really. Your sister would be quite alone, too, if you left her." She laughed and poured herself some more brandy. "But I said I was happy, right? Like hell I am!"

Snappy, wisecracking, sarcastic Mickey. Luz didn't know how to respond. Who would have guessed at the hurt Mickey kept hidden under that facade?

"Be smart, Luz. You grab on to your Mario good and tight, and love him like crazy, and then you fight hard to hang on to him for the rest of your life."

"My sister is a good person, and I know she loves me," Luz murmured, fighting to be as fair as possible.

"If your sister really loves you, then she'll be even happier when she sees you're happy. We're all good people, Luz, but we all make mistakes, right? Of course, there are exceptions."

"Chuck and Rita, you mean," Luz said. "I wonder what will happen to Rita now?"

"She'll survive. That kind always does, one way or another."

"Survive?" Luz shuddered. It was getting late, and she had taken up enough of Mickey's time. The woman looked haggard and worn out. Luz came over to her and hugged her. "Thanks, Mickey. Thanks for the brandy, the tissues, and for a few other things."

"You okay now?"

"Let's put it this way, I feel much better now than when I walked in that doorway a while ago," Luz assured her. She took up her purse. From the door she whispered, "Good night."

"Luz, I've been wanting to ask you something," Mickey blurted out just as Luz was about to leave.

"What is it?"

"Why hasn't your sister ever married?"

"I don't know." Luz was very surprised when she had to admit to that fact. "She's never talked about it." She managed to bring about a bright smile. " 'Night, Mickey."

On the way back home, Luz prayed that Trina had gone to bed. What had they left to say to one another? Tomorrow she would simply tell Trina that she wanted to marry Mario, and Trina would have to reconcile herself to the marriage. But Luz remembered that her brother, Arturo, would be coming to Los Angeles, and suddenly she felt depressed all over again. Would Mario have to go through another scene, this time with Arturo backing up Trina? How long would it take Mario before he became fed up with all this stupid squabbling? Tonight he had whispered that he loved her and wanted to marry her, and he had to say this with Trina standing right there. How romantic, Luz thought bitterly, and how embarrassing!

Trina hadn't gone to sleep. Luz found her waiting. She walked into her bedroom and sat down on the bed because her sister was sitting in Luz's favorite chair, the one by the window. What could they say to one another but harmful and hurtful things? "When will Arturo be coming?"

"As soon as he can get permission for a leave of absence from the bishop."

"I want to see my brother. I haven't seen him since I was a little girl, but do you think it's necessary for him to come here only because of Jorge's spiteful lies?" She wanted to scream out about Trina's own lies, but didn't.

Trina's eyes sought Luz's. "Lies? Tonight I saw with my own eyes that your brother has something to be worried about, just as I have. That"—she halted, unable to say Mario's name—"that *man* acted as if he owned you—and you were ecstatic just being in the same room with him!"

"Yes, that's true. I was ecstatic," Luz flung at her sister, "because I love him and I'm going to marry him. No, don't turn away from me," she insisted. "Look at me and listen to me. I love Mario and I want him. Do you understand what I'm saying?"

Trina couldn't keep the anguish from showing, and Luz, thoroughly exasperated, jumped up from the bed. "Oh, what's the use?" she said, and began to change from her jeans and sweater to her bathrobe.

"Jorge would have never acted that way. He's a gentleman."

"Jorge is a liar, and he's a dirty old hypocrite." Luz had taken enough, and she quickly shut off Trina's shocked objections. "Do you know what your precious Jorge tried to do to me, right here in your own house? While you were in the kitchen that night and I was 'entertaining' that worm in the living room, he decided to try to 'entertain' himself by kissing me and pawing me with his disgusting hands. I didn't scream because I didn't want to upset *you.* I didn't want you to know." Luz rushed over to her sister, forcing the woman to look at her. "If you hadn't been in the house that night, do you know what that 'gentleman' would have done to me? If I had been alone with him, he would have raped me!" She should have stopped speaking, but the more Trina twisted away from Luz's sudden grasp, the more inflamed Luz became. "Do you understand what I'm saying? Do you still want to force me to marry Jorge?"

With a gesture pathetically similar to the one Luz had used earlier when she, too, had begun to cry, Trina buried her face in her hands.

"Don't just cry and say nothing! Tell me you understand," Luz demanded, tearing Trina's hands away from her face. But there were no tears and no sobs. Instead, Luz saw something much worse etched in her sister's tragic brown eyes, something that drove her to kneel swiftly, and embrace the older woman. "Trina . . . Trina . . . !"

Trying as hard as possible to overhear, straining to lean halfway out the window, Maria Lopez's face was a study in frustration. Lights had been burning late in the Rivas household next door on many a night since Mrs. Lopez had spied young Luz Rivas passionately kissing that *very* handsome stranger a number of weeks ago. Mrs. Lopez had not missed one moment of the excitement that night, from the moment the roar of a powerful car's engine had awakened her from her innocent sleep, to the conversation and whispers in the yard, to Trina Rivas's discovery of the couple in the yard. Now *that* had been something! But— not half as good as when Jorge Garcia had chased young Luz around the living room, however. Mrs. Lopez had been mightily tempted to tell Trina Rivas all about that little episode, especially since relations had become rather cool between herself and Trina Rivas. It would serve her right because now Trina Rivas preferred to spend most of her time with Mrs. Campos who lived down the street— the same Mrs. Campos who had been forced to throw out her slutty daughter. Then, only this afternoon, the stranger had returned, and there had been a real hullabaloo next door. Mrs. Lopez screwed up her face in disgust. If only she could hear *something*. She was fuming! But the windows in the Rivas house were all shut tightly, and only the lights gave away the news that Trina and Luz Rivas were up talking the night away. With outraged indignation, Mrs. Lopez slammed down her own window, and went to bed. She spent the rest of the night utterly sleepless because the lights from the Rivas house burned bright until dawn.

CHAPTER EIGHT

"Top of the morning to you, Mr. Maldonado," the guard hailed Mario as he walked past the gate. "How are things with *you* today?"

"Fine, thanks." The guard seemed uncommonly jolly this morning, Mario thought; usually the old veteran greeted people with only a vague nod of his gray head.

The lot was teeming with activity and commotion. Unlike the normal workday hours at the studio's business offices, shooting began early in the morning at the lot, and Mario was already late. He had driven around for hours last night and had spent what was left of the evening wide awake, sitting in front of his iron fireplace, struggling with himself not to think. He had done nothing else but think. At dawn, he must have fallen asleep. He had awakened suddenly and found himself confronting dead ashes when the old firehouse clock tolled the hour that should have found him on his way to work. He had showered and dressed in minutes, and had probably stretched a number of traffic laws to the limit on the freeway in his mad dash to the lot, but he still arrived almost a half hour late. Walking swiftly through the lot to the sound stage he grimly recalled the occasional times he had been forced to remind a member of the crew that he would not tolerate preoccupation or tardiness, to interfere with work. But, perhaps, after today it wouldn't matter if he was preoccupied or not. After yesterday's run-in with Chuck, he might not even have a job.

One last obstacle separated him from reaching the sound-stage door, Lulu and her electric cart. Lulu dispensed bawdy humor along with coffee, rolls, and other assorted goodies around the lot for the many that just didn't have time to run to the commissary between "takes." Mario usually enjoyed joking with Lulu, but today he had no time, and little humor left in his soul.

"Hey, Mr. Maldonado, what's your rush? Don't you love me anymore?" Lulu had filled a cup with coffee and was holding it out to Mario.

"You know you'll always turn me on, Lulu, but . . ." What the hell! A few more minutes wouldn't make any difference, he realized, digging in his pockets for change.

"Oh, no, lover. Today your money's no good. Today, for you, everything is on the house. Everything, including me," Lulu winked. She must have been sixty, if she was a day, but Lulu still acted like a sex object.

"Just the coffee will be fine," he said, puzzled, "and I'll stand you for a few drinks one of these days."

"You're on! But here," she insisted, plunking a fresh cheese danish into Mario's hand, "eat! You need your strength."

Rather than to waste time wrangling over a cheese danish, he accepted the gift with a hasty smile and headed for the door. Juggling the coffee and the sticky roll, he walked into the sound stage.

The usual chaos reigned. Although filming crews always worked in the most casual atmosphere of any known business, someone in Mario's position always commanded special attention, and he was used to people calling out to him or saying hello. But today he noticed a subtle difference. People actually broke off conversations to say "Good morning," or "Hello," or "Hi, Mario" as he passed by. What had gotten into everybody? Then it hit him. *Chuck!* A hyped-up account of his fracas with Chuck must have spread like fire from Mercury's office to the lot. He felt his temper getting high about being admired for doing something he himself considered demeaning and dehumanizing.

About the last straw was seeing Mickey on the set. She was wearing a very motherly expression. On her face, it looked ridiculous.

"What are you doing here?" he asked, dryly.

"I thought I'd treat you to a fancy lunch today," Mickey stammered, gulping out the first excuse that jumped into her mind.

"At seven-thirty in the morning?" He dropped the gooey cheese danish into her hand. "Here. If you're hungry, eat this." He saw in amazement that Mickey's lips pinched together, then began to quiver, and for one horrible moment he actually thought she would cry. He dropped the cup on something nearby. "Mickey, I'm sorry." He started to apologize when he saw Juanito standing motionless a few feet away. "Do me a favor, will you?"

"Sure, Mario, anything," Mickey rasped, angrily brushing away something from her eye.

"Get me something to wipe this mess off my hands. And don't rush."

"But . . ."

"Do as I say, please."

Mickey followed Mario's eyes to Juanito. "No, Mario, don't. He had nothing to do with it," she pleaded.

"Mickey!"

"Yes, sir." One last look and she hurried away.

Mario retrieved the discarded coffee and slowly sipped it. Cold now and bitter, the coffee did nothing to calm his nerves or clear his head. He waited, and saw Juanito slowly walk to him.

"Fueron puras mentiras. Nunca hablé con Harrison."

Mario sipped some more of the nauseating coffee. *"¿Nunca?"*

"Ni una palabra. Te lo juro, Mario!" In his anxiety to have Mario believe him as he swore he had never spoken even one word to Chuck Harrison, Juanito clutched at Mario's arm. Raising his eyebrow only a fraction, Mario looked down at Juanito's hand. Juanito quickly let go, bringing his hand down to form a fist at his side. "I know what everybody thinks," he seethed, glancing around the set. People stood about not looking at either of them, but the suspicion and contempt could be felt like a heavy hand across his face. "I don't care what other people think. It's being batted around that I fell in with Chuck's con job. I didn't, Mario, I swear it! I've never even talked to him about the script. Even if he had said something to me, I would have told him to ditch it. I love Luz, and I couldn't do her any dirt." He stammered, then spoke out clearly. "You're my friend, Mario. Why should I do that to you?"

Mario smiled, but there was absolutely no humor in his eyes. "You know, Juanito, that's exactly what I asked myself. I thought of a number of reasons, but I didn't want to believe any of them. I still don't."

Juanito stared at Mario quizzically. "Hey, friend, didn't anybody reach you at home last night?"

"I wasn't home for most of the evening. I drove up the coast to Malibu, had a drink, and then got home late."

"Nobody called you?"

"I pulled the phone jack out of the wall." Mario turned away and strolled a step or two. "Why?"

"After you left . . . ah . . . left Harrison's office . . . I mean, they took him to the hospital."

Mario's eyes narrowed as he looked back at Juanito. "How is he?"

"Believe it or not, okay." A gleam of respect sneaked into his eyes—which quickly disappeared when he saw

Mario's frown. "You're lucky you busted his nose and not his mouth."

"Why is that?" Mario asked sarcastically.

"Because after they released him and he went home, some of the studio's top brass talked things over with him. After they got statements from Mickey and Betsy, I mean. And from me. He came clean, Mario. He told them everything. And don't worry," Juanito laughed from sheer relief, "he won't be pressing any charges against you!"

"So he lied about you, too," Mario murmured, but Juanito clearly heard the regret in that sentence. And the apology. "I'm sick of hearing about Chuck Harrison. It's about time we all got to work." He walked to the edge of the set and told his assistant, "Let's get going."

Everyone on the set had been hanging back and waiting for something to happen, but as soon as Mario gave the signal, the tension broke like magic and work began.

Ten hours later, with a few short breaks to relieve the grind, Mario called it a day. He had found himself looking over his shoulder every other minute. Luz: he had been searching for her. This was no way to work. There was a phone nearby, but he had tried not to remember it existed. Some of the actors and crew mingled for a while, then slowly made their way out of the sound stage. Juanito and Mickey were exchanging a few words and seemed to be disagreeing about one or two things.

Mario picked up his jacket and was just about to leave when he saw Herb Bliss. *Well, this is it,* he thought.

"Do you have a moment to talk, Mario?" Herb Bliss was a very polite person and looked like a librarian, which was exactly what he had started out to be in life. But he had teethed on films. His father had been one of the industry's legendary figures, and after making a stand to preserve his own identity by studying to be a librarian, he had finally given up all that nonsense and was now where he

160

belonged. He headed up Mercury Studios. His mild appearance was deceiving; he had Bliss blood in his veins . . . and the instincts of a barracuda.

"Certainly," Mario answered, shaking the offered hand.

Bliss looked around like a blinking owl. "It's kind of stuffy and hot in here, isn't it? Would you like to go somewhere else to talk, Mario?"

"No, this is fine. I'm quite comfortable here." He dropped his jacket over the back of a chair and sat down. Out of the corner of his eye, he saw Mickey and Juanito standing as still as statues. What was Luz doing at this moment?

"That's Juanito Jimenez over there, isn't it? Would you mind if I asked him to join us?"

"No, of course not." He silently cursed himself for disconnecting the phone last night. Had she needed him, and tried to phone?

"Now we're all comfortable, aren't we?" Bliss blinked and looked happy.

Juanito had pulled up a chair, and Mickey had found a stack of papers that needed her immediate attention on the far side of the empty sound stage. "What did you want to talk about?" Mario asked rather impatiently. He could feel Juanito's nervousness and smiled at the kid, reassuringly.

"Mr. Harrison is no longer with our studio." Herb Bliss spoke softly and very clearly. "The unfortunate incident is closed, unless you wish to further pursue legal . . ."

"I didn't write that script, Luz Rivas did. You will have to take that matter up with her."

"Of course, Mario." Touchy, touchy, all of these artistic persons; handle carefully! "But will you tell her that we would very much like to buy her script?"

"I'll have my secretary contact her."

"Oh, that will do very nicely." He blinked at Mario

161

blandly once or twice, and then turned to Juanito. "I hear great reports about you, Juanito."

"I'm glad, Mr. Bliss. I've enjoyed working on this picture very much. I've especially liked working with Mario," he added meaningfully.

"Good. Would you be interested in reading Miss Rivas's script? For the lead, of course."

"If you shoot—will Mario be directing?"

"There wouldn't be another director in town I'd even consider," Bliss answered with his softest voice yet. Juanito grinned, then nodded, quickly.

"Then it's settled," Mario said, standing up and grabbing his jacket. "Thanks, Herb, but we can get to the details another day, can't we?"

"Of course. I must be going myself. Good-bye." Herb Bliss left as quietly as he had come.

Juanito let out a long, suppressed sigh. "Maybe you could be very cool, but I was shaking in my boots!"

"Don't ever admit that to anybody else. You, Juanito, are now on your way to being a 'star.' How does it feel?"

"I'm numb, man. Check with me in a couple of years."

Mario seemed in a hurry to move away, to get out of the sound stage all of a sudden. "Do me a favor, Juanito. Take Mickey out to whichever restaurant she wants for dinner, and buy her everything on the menu. Will you do that for me?"

"Sure," Juanito replied, "but aren't you happy about the script? Happy for Luz, I mean."

"Yeah." He turned and began to walk away.

"Mario?"

"What is it?"

"Oh, nothing, I guess. We can talk tomorrow. About the script, and about Luz?"

But Mario didn't seem to hear. He was gone in a second. Mickey shuffled over immediately. "What was that all about? Was Bliss upset? What did he say?" Juanito told her the wonderful news. "Beautiful," Mickey hooted.

"Mario wants me to take you to dinner. Name the place."

"Never mind dinner. What did he say about *Luz?*"

Juanito looked slightly embarrassed. "I didn't have the nerve to ask him."

"Didn't he call her last night?"

"I don't think so. He spent the night driving around."

Mickey made a face. "I could knock their heads together."

But Juanito was young enough to still show some of his enthusiasm. "Look, it's not going to help Mario and Luz if we starve, right? I'm hungry."

Mickey was about to say something nasty, but she didn't—not after seeing the glow in Juanito's handsome face. "Okay, let's you and me celebrate. And, Juanito, dinner is on me!"

It was as warm outside as it had been inside the sound stage. Mario shifted his jacket from his arm to his shoulder and looked around. The sun was still high on the horizon and its brightness blinded. Halfway down the "street" was a phone booth, and Mario strode over to it quickly before he changed his mind.

"Good afternoon, this is Miss Luger speaking." Betsy sounded extra peppy and perky for so late in the afternoon, but she also sounded as if she had been munching on something when the phone had rung.

"It's bad manners to talk with your mouth full, didn't you know that?"

"Mario! Oh, my gosh, everybody's talking about you here at the studio. You're the sensation of the year! Wait a minute, let me wash down this *cuerno* with something here . . ."

A *cuerno* was a Mexican pastry; so Luz had been to

work today. Mario felt anxiety clutch at every muscle in his body.

". . . yeah, so I was saying . . ."

"Betsy, just a moment," Mario interrupted. "Is Luz there?"

"No, she's not. I really haven't seen her too much today. She's been to all kinds of meetings that have lasted for hours and hours . . ."

"Betsy, please, do you know where she is now? Can I reach her anywhere?" She was in one of her infuriatingly flighty moods, and Mario tried to keep his tension in check.

"No, I don't," Betsy wailed. "She just stuck her head in the door about thirty minutes ago and said she was leaving."

"All right, Betsy, thanks . . ."

"Mario, wait, don't hang up. Is there a message? I mean—if she should call in before I go home, is there anything you want me to tell her?"

"No." This time he rang off before she could ask any more questions. He thought again about the phone on the sound stage and bitterly cursed himself for being a complete and total fool.

Stalking off toward his car, he retraced his steps past the sound stage and saw Luz standing motionless in the large doorway. She had seen him, too. He had never fully realized how fragile she could look. She had on something white and soft and very feminine, and her wide dark eyes in her lovely face only added to that air of vulnerability that had so captivated him from the first time he had seen her. But when she came to him, she was a woman determined, assured, and unmistakably in love.

"Nobody in there could tell me where you had gone . . ."

"I just called your office, and Betsy didn't know where you were . . ."

164

They both spoke at the same time, and neither of them were saying what they wanted and needed so desperately to say to one another. They were standing right in the middle of the small road, and people scooted and zigzagged around them from both directions. He pulled her away from the crowd and down along a sidepath that opened onto an outdoor set of a turn-of-the-century park square. It had elm trees and wrought-iron benches and filigreed canopies; it was also quite deserted.

For minutes they just clung to each other. However, long afterward, Luz tried to speak, no matter how breathlessly. "If I hadn't found you exactly when I did, I think I would have quite truthfully gone out of my mind."

"I wasn't in much better shape," he admitted, low and caressing. "Why didn't you call me?"

"I didn't just want to tell you how I felt over the phone, and I couldn't break away from the office any sooner. It's a madhouse."

"I've had a busy day, too." He kissed her with a lightness this time. "Luz, I have some great news for you. Herb Bliss came to see me on the set." He told her everything, and watched her emotions run the gamut from gratitude, to pride, to sheer exuberance. She nestled deeper in his arms. "I was so worried that your career would be damaged. Ah, Mario, do you know how much I love you?"

"Convince me."

"Here?" Her mouth curved up in the corners.

"Anywhere," he murmured, then pulled back to look at her again. "You and Trina. How is it between you?"

"We spent the night talking, really understanding each other for the first time in our lives together."

"Do you want to tell me about it? You don't have to, you know."

"I must," she pleaded, "because then you'll understand her, too, and that's very important to me, darling." But she had to kiss him once more before she said, "I thought

165

she had never loved anybody in her life. I mean, loved somebody the way I love you. Oh, I was so wrong."

He held her strongly and concentrated on every word. "There was someone then—someone you never met?"

"Yes. He was an American, drifting through Mexico, part artist, part poet, and all dreamer. Trina was young in every way. She fell in love with him, and she still wants to believe that he loved her—just a little bit." Luz felt Mario's arms convulse tighter; she knew exactly what he meant by that gesture. "One day, he was gone. She knew he would never return to her . . . so she set out to find him. He had told her that he was born here in L.A. and had given her a home address in this city. She lied to my parents, telling them she was merely going to a larger village nearby to find work. She left knowing she could never return home again. It took her weeks to get here, and when she tried to find the address he had given her, she found there was no such address . . . and there never had been. She never saw him again." Mario had begun to stroke her hair, very softly. "Eventually she got a job at the bakery, and the rest you know."

"Afterward, she never thought of marrying anyone else?"

"She couldn't. She still loves him."

"God, I'm sorry, darling," he whispered. "I had some pretty strong feelings against her."

"I did, too, for a few moments."

"How was she found? I mean later, when you were sent to her from Mexico?"

"She never dared write home, but eventually she did write my brother at the seminary . . ." She gasped and stiffened against him. "What time is it?"

"After six. Why?"

"Arturo called this morning." Luz jumped up from the bench. "He was notified only yesterday that he had been

166

granted special leave. His plane will be landing in less than an hour at L.A. International!"

"Luz," Mario called to her, catching her by the hand as she was ready to run off, "I'll drive you to the airport."

"Oh, I'm so glad. But—are you sure you want to meet him so soon after what you went through last night?"

His laughter brushed away all her doubts.

All highways leading to the airport complex were jammed with traffic. The huge parking areas were also jammed. Luckily, Mario found an empty spot not too far from the terminal after only driving once around the parking area loop. Hand in hand, they dashed across the traffic lanes and Luz glanced up at the "Arrivals" screen the second they ran into the terminal building. "The plane arrived early. We're a half hour late!"

"Come on," Mario urged. They didn't wait for the slow-moving slide walks to take them through the corridors that tunneled under the runways. Instead, they swiftly covered the distance by running alongside the belt, and by bounding up the stairs, ignoring the equally slow escalators. The huge jumbo jet was parked beyond the silver panes of glass enclosing the entire waiting area at the designated gate, and few people remained standing around.

Although she had not seen her brother since she was a child, Luz never hesitated. Mario watched as she flung herself into a man's arms, and he saw the man embrace her with matching joy. Padre Arturo Rivas was a downright surprise! Expecting a gray-haired priestly-looking gentleman in dark clothes and clerical collar, Mario saw instead a vigorous young man about his own age with the stamp of a person whose mission was not within walls but out in the fields under the open sky. His civilian clothes were as casual as the broad smile he was directing toward Mario; and his handshake, when offered, was warm yet strong. "So you're the man Luz couldn't stop talking about this morning on the phone?"

"I hope so." Mario returned the smile.

"How is our sister?" Arturo asked Luz.

"Today, fine. Yesterday . . ." Luz looked from her brother to Mario, then back again. "Do you think the three of us could spend a few minutes together before you talk to Trina?"

"I was about to suggest the same thing myself," Arturo nodded.

They found a secluded spot over in a corner of the lounge, and Arturo seated himself across from Mario. Luz sat close to Mario and slipped her hand into his hand. His hold tightened immediately.

"Do you know Trina well?" Arturo asked Mario.

"I've only met her twice, and then only for a few minutes. Both times, the sparks flew."

Arturo sighed and looked at Luz. "Let me explain about Jorge. Trina asked me to recommend someone for you to marry, assuring me that the customs in the Hispanic community here were exactly as those in Mexico. Neither Trina nor Jorge ever told me that you didn't wish to marry him. They made excuses—school, your age, and so forth. I had no reason to disbelieve either one of them. Why didn't you tell me the truth in your letters, Luz?"

"I was afraid." She smiled, now realizing her foolishness. "I didn't want to complain to you behind Trina's back, either. I guess I just hoped that Jorge would get discouraged and never return. But Trina went on reassuring him I would change my mind." Luz looked at her brother for the first time with anxiety. "You know why Trina yearned so desperately for me to marry Jorge, or somebody like him, don't you?"

He nodded sadly. "Yes, it's obvious. She didn't want you to fall in love and make the same mistake she made. She told me the real story just before I sent you to her. She asked my forgiveness and swore she would bring you up correctly. I suppose in a way she used you to ease her own conscience. She thought she was carrying out her *duty*."

"I never knew the real reason until last night." Another thing Luz and Trina had settled last night was that neither Mario nor Arturo would ever know the seamier side of Jorge's character. It was truly over, so why dredge up anything else against the pathetic rancher? She gazed at Mario imploringly. "Trina is a wonderful person, and I want you to know each other better. Please, Mario?"

Instead of answering Luz, however, Mario appealed directly to Arturo, that familiar sparkle in his eye. "Both your sisters are very difficult, strong-willed women, you know that, don't you?"

"So I have found out over the years," Arturo replied, laughing. "But if you dig back into your own background, you'll remember that the only way to handle this kind of situation is with old-fashioned Hispanic diplomacy. For instance, for the past number of months, I have been receiving some very contradictory letters from Los Angeles. The more insistent Trina's letters became about marrying Luz to Jorge, the more I read the simple truth in Luz's glowing letters about a wonderful person she had met who was helping her write a film script. Oh, yes, the letters were mostly about the writing, but I have learned to read the human spirit even though I am only a provincial priest. So my letters to Trina were consoling and sympathetic, while my advice to Luz was to pay strict attention to your instructions and guidance, Mario." He beamed like a successful conspirator. "However, I knew I would eventually have to come here in person to straighten it all out. You leave Trina to me!" A second after they had stopped laughing, banishing the tension forever, Arturo assumed a very serious stance mixed with a hint of shyness. "There's something you'll have to help me with, Mario."

"And what's that?" Mario asked,

"As Luz's brother, I suppose it's my duty to ask you, what are your intentions toward my little sister here?"

"Strictly honorable, I assure you." He looked at Luz when he added, "I love her, and I want to marry her just as soon as possible."

"Hm-m-m, as soon as possible? That will fit very well with my plans, also." Arturo looked from one to the other. Both appeared puzzled.

"What plans?" Mario asked.

"I should explain that I am very anxious to return to my people. Mine is a rural parish of ranches and farms, and although the population is not great in number, the distances are large. I am the only priest in the area, and I spend most of my time traveling around in my old reconverted Jeep or on horseback." His brown eyes, so alike to Luz's, showed his love for his life's work. "My labors are not all purely spiritual. I've spent many a night helping a rancher's prize cow through a calfing, and many a morning having my ears assaulted by the offkey voices of the children's choir, which I direct. So, even if it's in a small way, my people need me. If you will allow it, I would very much like to officiate at the celebration that will join you as man and wife before I leave this city and return home."

Luz's answer was immediate and unrestrained. She embraced her brother and whispered, "Thank you. That would be a beautiful gift."

"Mario?" he wanted to know.

"I think Luz has said it all. Thanks, Arturo."

Luz's near-giggle broke the moment of simple emotion. "Mario, you know what?" Now she laughed, and her merriment was infectious. "You've proposed twice, once in front of my sister, and now with my brother here. Do you realize you've never *directly* asked *me* to marry you?"

Luz kept insisting all through the hectic days that followed, "I want this to be the happiest wedding ever, and I forbid anybody to cry!" And so no one had wanted to spoil Luz's wedding, and nobody wept at the loveliest service imaginable. Nobody except Betsy, that is, and Betsy really couldn't help it. All the flowers just about did her in. The service was punctuated with the poor girl's sneezes.

Later, in Luz's bedroom, Mickey borrowed a few cubes from the ice bag perched atop Betsy's head, and plunked them into her own glass. "You poor sick kid," Mickey tried to console the prostrate girl. "What are you going to do at your own wedding?"

"I'll gladly suffer, believe me!" Betsy wailed, all red and puffy.

"Luz has gathered up all the flowers, down to the last petal, and has relegated them to the backyard. You should be feeling much better soon."

The door opened a crack, and Luz peeked in. "Oh, I didn't know you were in here, Mickey. I thought Betsy might need something." She still wore her simple white wedding dress, enhanced by a thin ribbon that held back her long hair.

Betsy propped herself up in the bed. "You're the prettiest bride in the world, Luz." A few sneezes later, she added, "And I think it was a great idea to have your reception right here in your sister's home."

"Yeah, but how come you didn't have something in a restaurant, or wherever people have receptions?" Mickey smirked, remembering her own numerous wedding feasts. "I got as far as scrambled eggs in a delicatessen once after one of my unions."

"A restaurant seemed so impersonal, somehow. Anyway, Mario knew it would please Trina so much." Luz smiled and sat down on the bed.

"I don't know how Mario did it, or what he did, but your sister actually glows whenever he happens to walk into the same room. Luz," Mickey swore, "she actually adores him. What happened?"

"Arturo helped," Luz confessed, "and Mario's charm did the rest. We sat down, the four of us, and talked and talked. Poor Mario, he has spent hours talking! Trina had to be handled very carefully, but she finally stopped being so stubborn."

"Did you tell her the good news about selling your script?" Mickey asked.

"Yes. I think that's when she decided that Mario had a future—and that I could have a secure future with him."

Their good-humored laughter rang out, and they were comfortable with each other. Each of the women mused over her own thoughts.

"You didn't tell your sister about Rita taking your script, or any of that business with Chuck, did you?"

"No, Mickey. What for? Trina might tell Mrs. Campos, and why make that poor woman suffer any more, especially about something that's ancient history?"

"What's happened to Rita?" Mickey shook the cubes in her drink. "Something dreadful, I hope."

"Nobody knows."

Betsy suddenly shot up straight. "Hey, I haven't sneezed for over a minute. I'm feeling much better."

"Good," Luz said. "Perhaps in a little while you can come into the dining room so that we can cut the cake. We've been waiting for you."

"You mean I've held up the whole reception?" Betsy rolled off the bed with all the grace of a felled log. "That's terrible! Let's go and cut it right now."

"No, Betsy, *you* don't get to cut the cake—the bride and groom do that," Mickey lectured, shaking her head. "Haven't you ever been to a wedding before?"

"I've avoided them like poison. I get depressed seeing other women getting married," she muttered.

"Come on," Luz, prompted, "before you start sneezing again."

Everyone was so happy to see Betsy again, the poor girl soon forgot about all her problems. Mario gravitated to Luz. "Darling, I think you're avoiding me," he teased. "Where have you been?"

"Coddling Betsy, but she's feeling better now. Ready to cut the cake?" Luz whispered. They gazed at each other. The happiness they each felt was too deep for ordinary words. Not now, not here. Mario simply reached and pulled her head gently down on his shoulder for a moment. Then he answered, "Yes. I think your sister has something up her sleeve because she's very anxious that we slice open that cake. Any ideas?"

"Yes, but please act very surprised, won't you?"

The wedding cake rested on the table alone and unobstructed by anything else as befitted a work of art. Trina was standing near the table with Arturo by her side. With his clerical collar, he looked older and much more reverent. He beamed at his sister and she smiled back, proudly. Trina had spent two days at the bakery doing nothing else but supervising the baking and decorating of the spectacular cake.

Mario joined hands with Luz and they prepared to cut into the many-tiered pastry, with Juanito standing by Mario and Mickey to the side of Luz. One sharp slice and the miracle was accomplished amid much applause. Mario protested, laughing, "You'd better take over the rest of the job, Luz."

She began to cut farther into the cake. Each guest received a slice . . . and each slice brought forth a lovely surprise.

Betsy poked around in her dish. "Say, there's something inside!"

Juanito had been watching her astonishment. "It's a Mexican custom that probably goes back to Indian times."

He was suddenly being watched by everybody, some who knew the lovely custom and some who didn't; and he felt very foolish about opening his mouth. "Well, at least—that's what my mother told me," he said, boyishly.

"Go on," Mario coaxed, "I'm beginning to remember some of the ritual myself."

"It's like telling fortunes. Whatever you find, that's what's going to happen to you the rest of your life. Even if you can't recognize it, you still have to find out what the gift means. Somebody who knows about things like that looks at the gifts, and reads the real meaning into it. The gifts are supposed to bring the person only good luck. Anyway," Juanito finished with a flourish, looking very relieved, "that's the way it was explained to me."

Mario's eyes met Arturo's. Both men were thinking the same thing. "Thank you," Mario smiled, turning to Trina. "You didn't forget anything, did you?"

"It's a lovely custom," Trina said, "and I wanted to keep it as a surprise for you and for Luz."

"Let's see what everyone received," Arturo said, separating his slice of cake. He brought forth a tiny ceramic violin. It was perfect in every detail, beautifully fashioned. "Ah, yes," he said, laughing in good humor, "to forever remind me of my screeching angels in my choir."

Mrs. Lopez, who had been honorably invited to the wedding so that she did not have to spend the day stretching her neck out of shape next door, was appointed to decipher the legends of the little toys. Each discovery brought happy, comical comments. Juanito's gift proved to be very perplexing. It was a miniature gold key.

"Of course, a key to a golden future," Luz suggested. There were howls protesting her corny predictions.

While everyone else at the *fiesta* was involved in playing the traditional wedding game, Arturo nodded to Mario, and they found a quiet corner in the kitchen to talk for a second.

"I would very much wish to have you and Luz come down to Jalisco to visit. It's been many years since she has seen the *pueblo* of her birth. I think Luz would enjoy visiting it again."

"I'm sure she would," Mario agreed. "I would very much like to travel in Mexico, myself. I've never been there." They both grinned at that fact, especially since they were speaking, very naturally and comfortably, in Spanish.

"It's good to renew old ties." Arturo had a matter of no small interest to discuss with Mario. "Did you know I'm taking Trina back home with me tomorrow?"

"No, I didn't!" Mario was very surprised. "I can't believe she'd want to return there."

"It's only for a short vacation, of course, but I think she'll have a wonderful time."

"How long will she be gone?"

"How long will you and Luz want to be completely by yourselves?"

Again their eyes met in mutual understanding. Luz, who had not been aware that Mario and Arturo had left the festivities, heard the sudden laughter erupting from somewhere on the other side of the house, and was enormously happy to know that her brother and her husband had turned out to be such good friends.

"Luz," Betsy cried, bounding up to her, "Mrs. Lopez can't seem to figure out my future, at all! Maybe, you can help me . . ."

And so the party continued. Finally, many hours later, Luz went into her bedroom to change out of her lovely wedding dress into something much less formal. This being Southern California, where no occasion remained formal for *too* long, and remembering that they only had a short distance to travel, she put on a very casual pair of slacks and an old comfortable sweater. She also knew that

175

Mario was waiting impatiently by his car already, so she didn't fuss, changing quickly.

As Luz left her bedroom, she found Mrs. Campos waiting to speak to her. "A beautiful wedding, Luz," she said, hugging her tightly. "I wish you both so much good luck."

"Thank you so much." Luz expected to see some sadness in the woman's eyes, but she saw a gleam of hope, too.

"Rita called me this morning."

Luz couldn't explain why, but she still cared, cared very deeply. "What did she say? Where is she?"

"In New York. She sounded fine." Mrs. Campos's eyes shone. "I—I'm glad she called!"

"I am, too." Luz didn't want to ask if Chuck was with Rita; her mother looked happy, and that's all that mattered.

But Mrs. Campos herself brought up the subject. "She said to tell you she was there alone. She also said to tell you she was very happy for you and Mario. So . . . !"

Trina came rushing up to them. "You'd better hurry, dear. Mario is beginning to look angry." Now she sniffed, giving in to her emotions, at long last. "I wish you had time for a proper honeymoon."

"We will, very soon." She hugged her sister good-bye.

"But when? If you keep postponing it, you'll never go!"

"Mario's picture is just about finished. Then we can get away for a long vacation," Luz smiled.

She turned, and Arturo was walking toward her. "I'm so sorry you're leaving tomorrow. I wish . . ."

His brown eyes were filled with the satisfaction of a man who had very successfully accomplished an important mission. "Mario has promised me he will be bringing you home for a visit."

"Ah, that's a beautiful idea," Luz said, thrilled.

"You'll keep writing? I mean, both letters to me *and* scripts with Mario?"

"Yes, Arturo, I promise to do both."

"Now you'd better hurry," he insisted.

Luz had just run down the steps to Mario, who greeted her with badly concealed exasperation. "Don't you know it looks bad if the bride refuses to leave her own reception?" But the sparkle was there in his eyes.

"Why?" She knew he wasn't really angry.

"Everybody will think you're dreading the hours ahead, not wanting to be alone with me."

"Impossible!" She smiled a secret smile, and entwined her arms around his neck. "But just in case there should be any doubt in anybody's mind . . ." She kissed him long, and longingly, and there was no room for doubt in anyone's mind, least of all Mario's.

The kiss was interrupted by a shriek from Betsy. "Luz, you forgot to throw your bouquet!"

"Darling," Mario warned.

"Oh, Mario, it'll only take a moment—and I want to be sure Betsy's the one who catches the flowers," Luz laughed.

The irrepressible Mrs. Lopez leaped to the rescue, and handed Luz the small cluster of white roses she had carried in church. All the guests had congregated around the front door.

"All right, here goes." Just as the bouquet left her fingers, Luz remembered all of a sudden the unfortunate girl's aversion to even the tiniest blossom. "No!" she cried. "No, Betsy, don't *touch* the flowers!"

Somehow, Betsy ducked in time. But behind her, staggering to get out of the way, Mickey was not so lucky. The bride's bouquet dropped right into her hands. "No, oh, no, not again!"

Mario had to keep one hand on the wheel and the other on the stick shift to constantly change gears, but Luz bridged that little problem by sitting as close to him as possible, her arms wrapped around his waist and shoulders, her head nestled lovingly against his upper arm.

"Mm-m-m, I love you." She lifted her head proudly and looked back at him.

He slanted a glance down at her, his eyes flickering light through those dark lashes, his smile as swift and bright as the summer's sunshine. "That's good because I feel kind of strong about you, too."

"Just strong, huh?" she prodded, mischievously.

"That will do for now—unless you want me to drive this car right on over to the side of this freeway, and . . . !"

"Nope . . . I'll wait!" But she sent him a smile of a promise that was to come. Of what had always been there . . . just for him. "Mario?" she asked, cuddling even closer, "I forgot to ask you, what did you get as your fortune?"

"I'll give you one guess, but I'll bet it was the same as yours."

"Tell me!"

"I knew something would be different about our legends," he laughed.

The wind had become colder and wilder the nearer they got to the beach, and the speeding gusts were flinging his hair back from his angular, handsome face. There was something raw and wild about him, all at once, also. "There was no fortune."

She moved her head slightly from side to side; his arm beneath her face flexed excitingly with the movement. "Or in mine, either."

"What do you think it meant?" He turned sharply off the highway, and headed toward the ocean's edge. The sun disappeared behind a bank of soft, mauve summer fog; it seductively cushioned the air around them, and everything seemed more vibrant, and yet, more intimate.

"I think it meant we should make our own future."

"No limitations, right?"

"Exactly."

He nodded, but it was an absentminded move. He was bending all his attention to driving straight home. Just a turn or two later, he brought the racing car to a feverish stop in front of the firehouse.

"Come on," he whispered, pulling her out of the car with an easiness that didn't fool her at all. He shielded her against the turbulence of both wind and fog in the circle of his arms until they reached the entryway, then she broke loose and ran with joy into the beautiful house.

The huge paintings of the missing artist still clung to the walls exactly as remembered. "Hasn't he returned?" she asked, surprised, stopping on the first step of the oak stairway.

"No," he murmured, following her to the step. "He called a few weeks ago, saying he was on his way back." He traced the curve of her throat, first with his eyes, then with his strong fingers. "I told him to go on studying the Mayan ruins for another three months—*at least* another three months."

At the top of the stairs now, she saw that the lovely room appeared different. Looking up, she knew why. The sensuous fog was dimming the light away from the skylight. The room needed the sun.

She turned, and flung herself into his waiting arms. He lifted her in the air as he caught her to him.

"Tomorrow morning we'll look up and see . . . !"

"Tomorrow. But first, there's tonight."

She followed the patterns of light very closely, from the first thin thrust of the new day's sun until later, when the bright glow filled the room with gorgeous warmth. Not capable of moving too quickly, or truthfully not even wanting to move at all, she nevertheless found the strength to sweep her fingers rather indolently across the soft surface of the pillow and gathered together the feathery mass

179

of her hair. Unknowingly, a Gioconda-like smile settled around the corners of her beautiful full mouth. She turned her head ever so slightly and glanced across the bed to where Mario should have been sleeping. She knew she wouldn't find him there next to her, of course. He had first tried to leave just after the dawn, whispering solicitously, "No, don't move. Sleep. I'll be back soon, *mi vida.*"

But she hadn't wanted him to leave. "Stay . . . stay with me." Instantly, the urge to touch again, to hold each other again, to be one likeness again, returned with insane force, and he had lingered.

Now, twisting slowly over on her side, Luz let her body rest upon the place where Mario had reclined earlier, immersing herself completely in the still-warm hollow. Indulging her senses, recapturing the many moments of the night, she lay there for a while. *I love and I'm loved,* she kept repeating to herself; it was an overwhelming fact.

Startled, Luz pulled herself away from the warmth of the bed. She realized she must have dozed off. "Mario?"

No answer. The room was quiet. The sunlight seemed to be scolding her for her laziness. Catching up the fluffy comforter that had been pushed onto the floor sometime during the evening, she slipped from the bed and draped the bedcover around her body. A fresh, cold breeze beckoned from an open window overlooking the beach, and she hurried across the room to sit before the window and gaze out beyond.

The morning was still very young. Nobody strolled along the beach, but down by the water's edge a man came slowly out from the surf and walked toward the sands. In spite of the distance, Luz recognized Mario immediately. He walked with that easy grace, that bold assurance that was uniquely *his* way. As he came closer and closer to the firehouse, rubbing himself down vigorously with a towel, Luz marveled again at the spirit of fierce independence that was such an important part of his character. She

180

leaned her face against the cool pane, and wondered, What will it really mean to be Mario Maldonado's wife?

Luz remained at the window, deep in thought. And that's exactly how Mario found her. "Is that sudden regret I see on your beautiful face, Mrs. Maldonado?"

She had to smile at the tiny touch of fear in his voice. "No, my darling, there is absolutely no regret. I have never been so happy in my life."

"Are you sure?"

"Yes."

"Then tell me why you were gazing so wistfully out of that window."

"I was gazing at you," she admitted freely. "I was watching the way you walked, and the way you moved. I was falling in love with you all over again."

He covered the distance between them quickly. When he knelt beside her she swiftly turned to capture him to her. Then the comforter slipped aside, and now nothing hindered their mingling.

She shivered a little. "The water was very cold this morning, wasn't it? Your skin feels so cool."

His lips moved against her. "Warm me," he whispered. As her small hands began to stroke and circle a provocative pattern that traveled across his back, then moved to his shoulders, and then descended down his chest, he moaned teasingly, "Quite an expert at this sort of thing, aren't you?"

"Of course." The undulating movements never ceased.

Mario pulled his head back. "Exactly what do you mean by 'of course,' Luz?" The tease had left his voice, and there was more than a bit of fire in his dark eyes.

"Oh, I just meant that I've learned from all my lovers . . ."

"*All* your lovers?"

"Yes. I've had dozens and dozens of them."

"Luz!"

It was time to stop torturing him, she knew, but a little of the devil in her spirit cajoled her to go on with this outrageous lie. "My poor darling, didn't you guess I had led a scandalous life before we met?"

"No."

She could have very easily kept up this vexing little game because his obvious surprise was slowly turning into a burning jealousy—and what woman did not secretly yearn to incite a smidgen of jealousy from the man she loved as a sure sign of his complete adoration? But this silly, innocent feminine diversion was becoming dangerous.

Although he had remained in her arms, Mario was now silent and motionless. Where before he had felt merely cool to her touch, he now radiated an almost unearthly coldness. "Luz?"

The raw question in his voice was answered swiftly and forever by what he saw in her eyes. Between them passed a message so intense, so strong, that it left both of them quite shaken.

"I must be going crazy—but I love you more and more every second."

"Is this how it will continue to be with us, Mario?"

"Yes." He left the amorous curve of her arms and reached down for the forgotten comforter and, tenderly and protectively, he wrapped his wife within its folds. "Yes, this is how it will always be with us. I promise."

Thoughts about tomorrow intruded, then were deliberately brushed aside. "I don't ever want to leave this room!" The words cascaded out all in a rush. She laughed, insisting impulsively, "Let's stay here—forever—together!"

"Fine with me," Mario said, joining in with her laughter. "I don't mind starving to death, but I'd feel damned guilty about being responsible for my whole crew at the

182

studio going hungry while I spend the rest of my life making love to you—instead of working."

"You'll just have to choose," she mocked, "between me and your work."

"Let them starve," he decided immediately, noticing that the comforter had begun to fall slowly to the floor again. There was a spot right beneath one of her small but lovely breasts that *had* to be kissed. "And I don't feel the least bit guilty . . ."

But she had remembered something important. Entwining her fingers deeply into his thick black hair she forced his head back and looked down at him. "As a matter of fact, darling, I'll have to return to the studio myself for a few days."

Seeing she was quite serious, he leaned away from her with a sigh. "Why? I thought you were through with your job there. What about your writing?"

"I'll go on with my writing, but I have to help Betsy."

"Betsy? How?"

"I recommended Betsy for my position, and they gave her the job. Only, I left a lot of unfinished work . . ."

"And you want to help her get off to a good start, right?"

"Yes. Do you mind very much?"

"No, not at all. But I want you to start on your next script as soon as possible. How long will it take you to clear things up at Mercury?"

"Only about a week, or so. By then you should be finished filming, won't you?"

"I should be, if we keep to schedule."

"You see, it'll work out beautifully! Oh, Mario, then we won't have to wait a long time to go on our honeymoon in Mexico. Remember, you promised." She searched his face eagerly. "You haven't forgotten, have you?"

"How could I forget?" he replied with a small smile

183

playing around his mouth. "I promised your brother, didn't I?"

She frowned prettily at his little joke, then quickly got all caught up in visions of their dream vacation. "There are so many places I want to see . . ."

"Good. I'll leave all the planning to you." He was actually much more interested in the fact that Luz had wriggled quite free of the blanket in her excitement over their forthcoming *luna de miel*. It became impossible for him not to crave to caress the roundness of her hip, right there, where it dipped and curved and blended into the heat of her thighs; what his eyes hungrily feasted upon his hands soon claimed. "Now that everything's been settled . . ."

"Mario, no!" Luz jumped up laughing and slithered just beyond his grasp. "I have a million things to do if we're going to be leaving on our trip so soon." She ran lightly across the room.

"Hey, wait!" He followed quickly enough. "Only a few minutes ago you were begging me to stay here with you forever. Now you're running away from me. Where are you going?"

"Don't worry, I'm only going to take a shower, I want to soak in hot water for at least an hour!"

"And what shall I do while you're indulging yourself in such selfish pleasure?"

"You could be a real darling, and brew some of your wonderful coffee, couldn't you?" She had reached the shower, smiling a coquettish appeal. "Pretty please?"

"I could," he conceded, coming closer, catching her around the waist, and trapping her within the closeness of the shower stall. "But I'll need a little coaxing."

"Mario . . . !"

"Stop squirming . . ."

"Darling . . . !"

"If you don't stop struggling I'll turn on the cold water

full blast, I'm warning you." She stopped all resistance at once, knowing he meant what he said, succumbing to his command with a sexy little moan that instantly propelled every red corpuscle in his body to explode, and then furiously fuse. "Tell me . . . just how much do you really want that coffee?"

"M-m-m-m, *very, very* much . . ."

"Well then . . . show me . . ."

The almost sensual smell of the fresh coffee permeated the room. Mario turned around as Luz approached, sensing her nearness. She was constrained to smile at his nearly improbable handsomeness. He wore white with spectacular results; his tawny skin and dark hair dazzled in contrast to the snowy shirt and cords in which he was now casually dressed. He continued to drink slowly from a large mug held tightly in his hands. A smaller cup of the same design waited for her on a side table, filled almost to the top with the dark, rich liquid. She tasted the coffee carefully because it was still very hot. "It's even better than I remember."

"I was truly inspired."

"Well, I feel inspired, too," she confessed, responding to the knowing glint in his eye, "and if you'll just give me a moment to find where you keep things in your kitchen, I'll cook you a first-rate breakfast."

"Absolutely not," he laughed. "I don't want it to get around town that I forced you into housework the morning after our wedding night! No, instead, let's have breakfast at that place down the beach you liked so much, okay?"

"You mean in the library?"

"Yes. Remember?"

"Of course, I remember." She couldn't resist him anything. "Yes, let's! But only if you promise to let me cook you a superb supper tonight right here in your . . ."

185

"Luz, darling, listen to me," he said all at once, voicing something he had obviously been mulling around in his mind for a while. "I know you feel this is 'my' apartment, but don't you think you should start thinking about this place as 'our' apartment? Unless you'd like us to move somewhere else, of course. You know, we've never really talked about this."

Even as he suggested moving away he gave a hasty glance around, a glance so full of fondness and longing, unintentionally divulging how much he really loved this place. Luz thought of the joy he received from his early-morning swimming, and also of the free and careless life-style that was so much a part of his happiness. "You really love living here, don't you?"

"Yes, but I wouldn't give it a second thought if we decided to live elsewhere."

"Some other place . . ." she murmured, naturally thinking back to her life in the *barrio*. The familiar streets. The friends and neighbors. But that was her life before she had met Mario. *That* part of her life was finished forever. Rita would have thought that way. Rita . . . "No," she said, "no, there's no other place I'd like to live."

"Are you absolutely sure, darling?"

"Of course."

He finished his coffee, put aside the cup, then held her to him tightly. "There might be a problem, you know."

"What problem?"

"Well, we'll both be working here."

Yes, that could be a problem, but she asked, puzzled, "What about your beautiful new office at the studio? Won't you be doing most of your work there?"

"No, I don't think so." Her coffee cup was being crushed between them; he put that away, too. "I can only think clearly when I'm by myself, and I find I can't really get too much writing done in that magnificent office of mine." He grinned down at her. "Mickey tries her best to

186

buffer the chronic chaos at the studio, but it still bothers me—I just can't seem to get any creative work done there! I suppose what I'm saying is that I'll never be comfortable being part of the so-called establishment." Softly brushing a kiss across the top of her head, he wondered, "Do you mind being married to a maverick?"

"Not one bit," she vowed, pressing herself desperately harder against his chest and shoulders. "I relish it." However, the problem of working space still existed. "This room is so lovely, but it's certainly not large enough to hold *two* temperamental artists. We would be screaming at each other in less than an hour!" She didn't lose sight of the humor of the situation, but she also recognized it could prove serious. "What's the solution, Mario?"

"I have an idea. We would have enough room if we had the whole firehouse to ourselves, wouldn't we?"

"But—that's impossible! What about that artist fellow downstairs?"

"Just before he went off to Yucatan he mentioned he would probably be looking for a new place—a much, much larger place—soon after his return. I'm positive he'll be needing a really *huge* studio to store his paintings after studying the Maya!" Both his smile and optimism were infectious. "We could fix up the floor downstairs, and each of us could have our own private den. That way," he said, nuzzling the very tip of her nose, "*you* won't turn into a nag and drive *me* from the house."

"I could never nag . . . only inspire . . . remember?"

"How the hell can I forget . . ."

"Oh, Mario, it's a perfect idea," she cried, joyously.

Her outburst made him feel protective all over again. "We could buy this old firehouse, you know. Would you like that, my darling?"

"Yes! Oh, *yes.*"

"On one condition, however."

"I'm ready and willing to listen to anything within

187

reason," she said, stealing one kiss and then another. "What is it?"

"Downstairs we can have separate offices, locked doors, and tall walls. Okay, so much for sanity, privacy, and all that other stuff. But up here—up here there will never be any doors or walls between us, do you understand?"

"Ah, my darling, not only do I understand, but I absolutely insist we keep to that agreement!"

"Good. You know something? This relationship may work, after all! Now, I think it's much too late for breakfast, so-o-o, may I invite you to lunch, Mrs. Maldonado?"

"I accept gladly. I'm starving!"

They hurried down the oak staircase hand-in-hand, and stopped at the bottom as if by mutual consent. They suddenly realized they were looking upon the lovely old firehouse for the first time. Now it was their *home*. A moment later Mario led Luz through the front door. He hesitated, his hand still on the door handle, wondering if he should lock the front door.

But Luz had made her decision. "No, leave it open, Mario. Everything is perfect the way it is."

LOOK FOR NEXT MONTH'S
CANDLELIGHT ECSTASY ROMANCES:

16 BESIEGED BY LOVE *by Maryann Young*

17 WAGERED WEEKEND *by Jayne Castle*

18 SWEET EMBER *by Bonnie Drake*

Love—the way you want it!

Candlelight Romances

			TITLE NO.
☐ A MAN OF HER CHOOSING by Nina Pykare	$1.50	#554	(15133-3)
☐ PASSING FANCY by Mary Linn Roby	$1.50	#555	(16770-1)
☐ THE DEMON COUNT by Anne Stuart	$1.25	#557	(11906-5)
☐ WHERE SHADOWS LINGER by Janis Susan May	$1.25	#556	(19777-5)
☐ OMEN FOR LOVE by Esther Boyd	$1.25	#552	(16108-8)
☐ MAYBE TOMORROW by Marie Pershing	$1.25	#553	(14909-6)
☐ LOVE IN DISGUISE by Nina Pykare	$1.50	#548	(15229-1)
☐ THE RUNAWAY HEIRESS by Lillian Cheatham	$1.50	#549	(18083-X)
☐ HOME TO THE HIGHLANDS by Jessica Eliot	$1.25	#550	(13104-9)
☐ DARK LEGACY by Candace Connell	$1.25	#551	(11771-2)
☐ LEGACY OF THE HEART by Lorena McCourtney	$1.25	#546	(15645-9)
☐ THE SLEEPING HEIRESS by Phyllis Taylor Pianka	$1.50	#543	(17551-8)
☐ DAISY by Jennie Tremaine	$1.50	#542	(11683-X)
☐ RING THE BELL SOFTLY by Margaret James	$1.25	#545	(17626-3)
☐ GUARDIAN OF INNOCENCE by Judy Boynton	$1.25	#544	(11862-X)
☐ THE LONG ENCHANTMENT by Helen Nuelle	$1.25	#540	(15407-3)
☐ SECRET LONGINGS by Nancy Kennedy	$1.25	#541	(17609-3)

At your local bookstore or use this handy coupon for ordering:

Dell	**DELL BOOKS** **P.O. BOX 1000, PINEBROOK, N.J. 07058**

Please send me the books I have checked above. I am enclosing $ _____
(please add 75¢ per copy to cover postage and handling). Send check or money order—no cash or C.O.D.'s. Please allow up to 8 weeks for shipment.

Mr/Mrs/Miss _____

Address _____

City _____ State/Zip _____

Dell Bestsellers

- [ ] **RANDOM WINDS** by Belva Plain $3.50 (17158-X)
- [ ] **MEN IN LOVE** by Nancy Friday $3.50 (15404-9)
- [ ] **JAILBIRD** by Kurt Vonnegut $3.25 (15447-2)
- [ ] **LOVE: Poems** by Danielle Steel $2.50 (15377-8)
- [ ] **SHOGUN** by James Clavell $3.5Q (17800-2)
- [ ] **WILL** by G. Gordon Liddy $3.50 (09666-9)
- [ ] **THE ESTABLISHMENT** by Howard Fast.......$3.25 (12296-1)
- [ ] **LIGHT OF LOVE** by Barbara Cartland $2.50 (15402-2)
- [ ] **SERPENTINE** by Thomas Thompson $3.50 (17611-5)
- [ ] **MY MOTHER/MY SELF** by Nancy Friday $3.25 (15663-7)
- [ ] **EVERGREEN** by Belva Plain $3.50 (13278-9)
- [ ] **THE WINDSOR STORY**
      by J. Bryan III & Charles J.V. Murphy $3.75 (19346-X)
- [ ] **THE PROUD HUNTER** by Marianne Harvey ..$3.25 (17098-2)
- [ ] **HIT ME WITH A RAINBOW**
      by James Kirkwood $3.25 (13622-9)
- [ ] **MIDNIGHT MOVIES** by David Kaufelt $2.75 (15728-5)
- [ ] **THE DEBRIEFING** by Robert Litell $2.75 (01873-5)
- [ ] **SHAMAN'S DAUGHTER** by Nan Salerno
      & Rosamond Vanderburgh $3.25 (17863-0)
- [ ] **WOMAN OF TEXAS** by R.T. Stevens $2.95 (19555-1)
- [ ] **DEVIL'S LOVE** by Lane Harris $2.95 (11915-4)

At your local bookstore or use this handy coupon for ordering:

Dell **DELL BOOKS**
P.O. BOX 1000, PINEBROOK, N.J. 07058

Please send me the books I have checked above. I am enclosing $ _____
(please add 75¢ per copy to cover postage and handling). Send check or money order—no cash or C.O.D.'s. Please allow up to 8 weeks for shipment.

Mr/Mrs/Miss _____

Address _____

City _____ State/Zip _____